John Parker Anderson, Richard Garnett

Life of Ralph Waldo Emerson

John Parker Anderson, Richard Garnett

Life of Ralph Waldo Emerson

ISBN/EAN: 9783337085285

Printed in Europe, USA, Canada, Australia, Japan

Cover: Foto ©Raphael Reischuk / pixelio.de

More available books at **www.hansebooks.com**

"Great Writers."

EDITED BY

PROFESSOR ERIC S. ROBERTSON, M.A.

LIFE OF EMERSON.

·LIFE

OF

RALPH WALDO ·EMERSON·

BY

RICHARD GARNETT, L.L.D.

LONDON
WALTER SCOTT, 24 WARWICK LANE
NEW YORK : THOMAS WHITTAKER
TORONTO : W. J. GAGE & CO.
1888

CONTENTS.

CHAPTER I.

CHAPTER II.

CHAPTER III.

CHAPTER IV.

CHAPTER V.

CHAPTER VI.

CHAPTER VII.

CHAPTER VIII.

NOTE.

—⁍—

EMERSON has dealt severely with his biographers. With full knowledge that his history must be written, he thought fit to lead a life devoid of incident, of nearly untroubled happiness, and of absolute conformity to the moral law. His correspondence is seldom very interesting, and his diary is out of reach. The injured biographer must rely on whatever charm may attach to the not too frequent figure of one who lived as he wrote. His main dependence for matters of fact must repose on Mr. J. E. Cabot, Emerson's literary executor and authorized historian, whose consummate knowledge unfortunately for the above-mentioned biographer) is only rivalled by his consummate discretion. Cordial acknowledgments are also due to preceding writers—Mr. Ireland, Dr. Holmes, Mr. Cooke, Mr. Conway—whose works, if superseded as records of circumstance, are yet fresh with the aroma of the admiring love which led them to preoccupy the ground. Apart from these common obligations, the writer is specially indebted to the friend who prepared his index, and the friends who revised his proofs.

April 27, 1888.

LIFE OF EMERSON.

CHAPTER I.

ON May 25, 1803, William Emerson, minister of the First Church in Boston, was among the listeners to the Election Sermon preached "to great acceptance," by the Rev. Mr. Puffer. Whether he had left home in spite of inward monitions that he ought to remain, we are not informed; but, if misgivings he had, they were insufficient to prevent his presence at the dinner at Governor Strong's, in which the observance of the day culminated. While sitting at the Governor's table, his enjoyment of the repast was enhanced or interrupted by the tidings of an increase to his family: Ralph Waldo Emerson, William's fourth child and third son, having meanwhile been added to the population of Boston, "within a kite-string of the birthplace of Benjamin Franklin." The usual hour of dinner was then one. Ten hours sooner, allowing for the difference of Greenwich and Boston time, Old England had been enriched by the birth of

another child destined to wide literary renown, but
otherwise as dissimilar from the American as one man
of genius can be from another.   Edward Lytton Bulwer
was also born on May 25, 1803. Six years later the
coincidence was to be renewed by the birth on the same
day, on opposite sides of the Atlantic, of two great men
with infinitely more in common—Darwin and Abraham
Lincoln.

In one respect, nevertheless, the American and the
British infant agreed, they were both examples of the per-
sistence of family character, exemplifying the saying of
the former that "every man is a bundle of his ancestors."
Each of them, also, was destined to lose his father at an
early age, and each, while preserving the paternal type,
was more directly indebted to the care and guidance of a
wise and resolute mother.   Goethe traces the strict and
sober elements of his character to the paternal, the sunny
and genial to the maternal parent :

> " Vom Vater hab' ich die Statur,
>   Des Lebens ernstes Führen ;
> Vom Mutterchen die Frohnatur'
>   Und Lust zu fabuliren."

With Emerson it was the reverse.   Such animal spirits
as he could boast were derived from his father : the
higher and rarer elements of character from a mother
" whose mind had set its stamp upon manners of peculiar
softness and natural grace and quiet dignity." The
father was indeed a clergyman, and not too obviously
deficient in the staidness becoming the clerical character ;
but, genial and social, more of a moralist than a divine,

rather a man of letters than a man of learning, he re-presented a character notably modified since the time that its prototypes had crossed the Atlantic.

The name of Emerson, originating in the county of Durham or York, and celebrated in England as that of an eminent and eccentric mathematician, is not uncommon in the Northern States, and has been borne by several persons of note unconnected with the philosopher of Concord, among them a distinguished physician and a distinguished agriculturist. The first American settler of the name was Thomas Emerson, who arrived in Massachusetts about 1635. This ancestor of a line of dispensers of the bread of life had himself only dispensed the bread which perisheth to the people of Ipswich, but from the strong clerical bent evinced by his descendants it may be reasonably concluded that he was among those who forsook their native land for conscience' sake. The next lineal ancestor of Ralph Waldo Emerson was Thomas's son Joseph, " the pioneer minister of Mendon, who barely escaped with his life when the village was destroyed by the Indians." His wife, Elizabeth Bulkeley, was the most distinguished by descent of any among Emerson's ancestors, and may well have infused a new spirit into the family. She was great-granddaughter and granddaughter of successive rectors of Odell, in Bedfordshire—Edward and Peter Bulkeley, scions of the family of Bulkeley, or Buckley, in Cheshire. Edward was a staunch Puritan, author of a little black-letter volume dedicated to Walsingham, upbraiding the Jesuits for forsaking " the originall fountaine of the Greek wherein the Spirit of God did indite the Gospell," for a Latin version. The inheritor of his living and his opinions fell upon evil days, if those days are evil which test a man's steadfastness to his principles. Edward Bulkeley's Puritanism had earned the patronage of Walsingham; Peter's elicited the wrath of Archbishop Laud. Compelled to acknowledge to Laud's Vicar-general, Sir Nathaniel Brent, that he never used the surplice in the pulpit or made the sign of the cross in baptism, he was incontinently suspended, and cited to the High Commission Court "if he reform not before." Whether he made appearance is not recorded; but next year (1635), having secretly realised his estate, considerable for those days, he crossed the Atlantic with all his family, and settled at Cambridge, the future seat of New England learning. Moving onward, after no long time he became by honest purchase from the Indians owner of considerable possessions by the lilied Musketaquit, or Meadow River, in New Hampshire, and founded and named the town destined to be famous to all ages as Concord. "There is no people," he said to his flock, "but will strive to excel in something. What can we excel in, if not in holiness?" Supreme over his people's bodies and souls, he spent the remainder of his days a Protestant Pope, a republican monarch, bequeathing, on his death in 1659, his dignities temporal and spiritual to his son Edward, a sickly and gentle scholar, father of the lady who in 1665 espoused Joseph Emerson. "In a certain sense," writes the Rev. John Brown, the biographer of Bunyan, "Bulkeley is the patron saint as well as the founder of Concord, and traces of him are to be met with on every side. Of a dozen ministers who since 1637 have preached in the parish church of the place, five were either Bulkeleys or Emersons."

Joseph Emerson's son Edward married Rebecca, daughter of Cornelius Waldo, from whom this " beloved " and certainly most picturesque name came into the family. One likes to think of it as derived from the patriarch of the Vaudois, as may well be the case, for it first appears in England in the reign of Elizabeth, doubtless brought by foreign refugees. Two Waldos were among the original founders of the East India Company. Edward's son Joseph, minister at Malden, who graduated at Harvard College in 1717, left a name as "a heroic scholar," "the greatest student in the country," says his granddaughter. His opinion that his son ought never to leave his lessons came near occasioning little William's death, but the mother's intercession and the necessity of attending to farm work rescued the lad. He prayed every night that none of his descendants might ever be rich, and the effectual fervent prayer of the righteous man has hitherto been found to avail. His wife, Mary Moody, was the daughter of Samuel Moody, celebrated for his eloquence, his self-forgetting charity—so forgetful indeed that he gave away his wife's shoes instead of his own,— and his relentless pursuit after "graceless sinners who ventured into the alehouse on Saturday night." William Emerson, son of the scholarly minister of Malden, seems to have imbibed more of his maternal grandfather's spirit than of his father's. Not only was he an impassioned and enthusiastic preacher, but when the War of Independence broke out in his own parish, his patriotic ardour hurried him as army chaplain into the ranks, where he was shortly carried off by a fever. The Old Manse at Concord, celebrated by Hawthorne, was built for him.

William Emerson, the offspring of his marriage with Phœbe Bliss, evinced, on the other hand, more affinity to his grandfather " the heroic scholar," than to his father the fervent preacher, though by no means deficient in oratorical gifts.   Left an orphan at an early age, he soon gained a protector in a step-father, the Rev. Ezra Ripley, whose character, curiously compounded of credulity and sagacity, was afterwards to be graphically painted by his step-grandson. Ere long William Emerson had to dispute his mother's affection with a rapidly increasing brood of young half-brothers and sisters. His own inclinations are said not to have tended towards the ministry, but his mother's wishes, reinforced by broad hints in his step-father's devotional exercises, prevailed with him, and after an alternate course of college study and school-keeping, he was (1792) ordained at the age of twenty-three, and settled at Harvard, a town twelve miles from Concord. The congregation was small and the income correspondent—three hundred and thirty-three dollars annually— to which in process of time it became necessary to add two hundred and fifty more as compensation for the deprecia-tion of the currency.   Being too poor to keep a horse, he was almost debarred from other society than that afforded by the village itself, a restricted circle of plain but friendly and hospitable people, more sympathetic with the young minister's musical tastes than with his literary aspirations.

In the case of a clergyman who sings and plays on the
bass viol, it excites no surprise, slenderness of means notwithstanding, to hear of " conversations on the subject of
matrimony." These occurred in June, 1796, and on
October 25th of that year William Emerson was united to
Ruth Haskins, of Boston, and brought her from the New
England metropolis to dwell in the little sequestered
hamlet among the woods and rocks. " We are poor
and cold," he wrote in his journal, " and have little meal,
and little wood, and little meat ; but, thank God, courage
enough."

The family of Ruth Haskins was by no means so distinguished as that of her bridegroom ; its origin, indeed, was
uncertain. It had boasted, however, a member of sterling
worth in her father, John Haskins : and her mother,
Hannah Upham, sprang from one of the good old New
England families, prolific of " selectmen, moderators of
town-meetings, members of the General Court, officers in
the militia, and deacons of the church." John Haskins,
differing from his wife in religious sentiment, was an
Episcopalian of an unusually staunch type. He had pro-
tested stoutly against the changes in the Liturgy of
King's Chapel, by which, as Clough subsequently expressed it, " the tails of the prayers had been cut off,'
and the congregation had become Unitarian. This had
happened in 1785, after the flight of the old royalist
rector and the larger portion of his flock, who disappeared
along with British supremacy in the year of Independence,
no more than British supremacy to return. Mr. Haskins
emigrated too, but only to Trinity Church, whither he was
accustomed to repair at the head of half his numerous

family, his wife leading a procession of the other half towards the Congregational Church in Park Street. All this notwithstanding, the veteran Churchman would have the heretical pastors in of a Sunday evening, and treat them with sangaree out of a silver tankard. All was good humour and mutual toleration, and an atmosphere was preparing singularly suitable for the special message of John Haskins's grandson, who celebrated his death (1814) in some boyish lines. He was indeed a man of great firm-. ness of character and sound practical wisdom, whose pithy sayings were current among his neighbours, and to whom men going down to the sea in ships entrusted their money in preference to the bank. His daughter Ruth would seem rather to have resembled her mother, and to have even surpassed her graciousness of temper and wifely and motherly diligence. "I do not remember," says Mrs. Bradford, William Emerson's ward, "ever to have seen her impatient, or to have heard her express dissatisfaction at any time." The serious, almost anxious, but finely spiritual countenance prefixed to Mr. D. G. Haskins's account of the family is, but for the dark liquid eyes and the expression as of one troubled about many things, wonderfully like Emerson's in its highest mood. "The original of Ralph Waldo," says Clough, describing her at the age of eighty-four; from her, too, he inherited the musical resonance of his voice. Mrs. Bradford contributes some traits prettily characteristic of the pastor's wife: how, whereas she was satisfied that the silver communion plate, though her special charge, should be cleaned under her inspection by the sexton, the minister's lawn bands must be ironed by no one but herself. "It was the custom at that time for settled ministers to wear bands and black silk gowns, and a plaited broad band of black silk round the waist. Mr. Emerson looked very handsome thus attired." Of Ralph Waldo's infancy Mrs. Bradford only recollects that he had a surprising memory; that his dress was at first yellow flannel, succeeded by dark blue nankeen; and that at an early age he contracted an evil habit of sucking his thumb, which Mrs. Emerson eradicated by making him wear a mitten.

If the pecuniary advantages of William Emerson's marriage were not conspicuous, he had nevertheless enlarged the circle of his acquaintance, and gained friends in the native city of his bride. It may have been through her connections that in 1799 he was invited to preach before the First Church in Boston "on the solemn occasion of choosing officers for the Ancient and Honourable Artillery Company." The discourse, set off by the preacher's handsome person, melodious voice, and agreeable manner, gave such satisfaction that within a week he was offered the pastorate of this important church. His own inclination could not be doubtful, but it was necessary to obtain a dismissal from his rural congregation. To this end the people of Harvard were apprised by the people of Boston that "the alarming attacks upon our holy religion by the Learned, the Witty, and the Wicked, especially in populous and seaport towns," rendered it indispensable that the light of men like Mr. Emerson should no longer be concealed under bushels, but that individuals thus luminous should be "invited and supported to convince and confound the wicked" (nothing is said of the learned and the witty) "by their arguments, and allure them by their amiable behaviour." The people of Harvard seem to have had no objection to detach their pastor as a reinforcement to the metropolis, but were exercised by the apprehension of having to pay his successor a better salary. As insurance against this contingency, they claimed thirteen hundred dollars. The Bostonians showed their real desire to secure Emerson by meeting this demand considerably more than half way. After a tedious negotiation a thousand dollars were paid, and the young minister entered upon his new sphere on September 22, 1799. He had, he afterwards told his half-brother, made up his mind to leave Harvard in any event, and had contemplated removal to Washington, where he would have endeavoured "to plant a church strictly on congregational principles ; in which there was to be no written confession of faith, no covenant, and no subscription whatever to articles as a term of communion." This bold liberalism foreshadows the subsequent conduct of his son, and is, moreover, conclusive as to the writer's own attitude towards the great intellectual change which was silently revolutionizing the theology of New England.

"We progress in such and such ways," said a member of an orthodox church to a Unitarian : "but how do you Unitarians progress ?" "By other churches adopting our principles while keeping their own names," was the answer. Unitarianism must certainly be allowed to resemble the Kingdom of Heaven in one respect : it cometh not with observation. It has always been the result of a slow and silent process, begun long ere suspected, and progressing unchallenged long after its tendency has become plain. Protest is idle, for the phenomenon has its roots deep in human nature, being in fact bottomed on the elementary fact that every generation must and will look at things human and divine in its own way, and that the only method of insuring the permanency of any particular mode of thought is to renounce the exercise of thought entirely. William Emerson, whose ancestors' Calvinism had not been extreme, had fallen in easily with the current of the time : but, though there was the stuff of a vigorous controversialist in him, circumstances did not require him to come prominently forward. There seems, indeed, to have been an indisposition on all hands to stir up religious strife ; until at length an apple of discord was thrown, or rather fell in obedience to the laws of nature, in the shape of a vacant Professorship of Divinity. The question whether a Unitarian could be appointed on a Calvinist foundation could not but lead to contention. It was decided in conformity with the precedent settled at the English Reformation, and the irritation of the orthodox party found vent in the establishment (1805) of the *Panoplist*, a journal in which the new views were violently combated, and their supporters assailed with personal animosity. This tone, however, was not adopted until the publication of Buckminster's collection of hymns in 1808, the year in which William Emerson was brought nigh unto death ; nor did he ever recover so far as to take an active part in ecclesiastical politics. The influences, therefore, that surrounded Ralph Emerson's cradle were far less controversial than might have been expected, and in the very year (1821) in which he quitted college, the conflict wore itself out, leaving as its principal literary monument the

classic works of the meekest of controversialists, William
Ellery Channing.   Most fortunate was its breaking out
for the young thinker, for whom orthodox and heterodox
conspired to clear the way : most fortunate also its subsi-
dence, or he would have run great risk of giving up to
sect what was meant for mankind.

The less William Emerson felt disposed to take a
prominent part in controversy, the more likely was his
mental activity to find vent in literature.   The Christian
Minister Society, established for the publication of tracts,
was founded and long actively promoted by him.   He
was a member of the Massachusetts Historical Society,
and also of the Philosophical Society, of which he seems
to have regarded himself as the founder, since he calls it
"the child of my brain."   But his chief enterprise was
the editorship of *The Monthly Anthology*, the journal of
the Anthology Club, of which he was vice-president.
Busy judges, rising barristers, influential clergymen, even
a future President, found time to contribute to this
magazine, which represented the best intellectual culture
of Boston, in that day conservative in literature as in
politics, and unforeboding of the mystic baptism which it
was to receive from the editor's little boy.   The deep
influence which Godwin had so recently exerted on the
one contemporary American of literary genius—Charles
Brockden Brown—found no echo among the Bostonian
literati: who had imagination enough to appreciate Scott's
romantic picturesqueness, but recoiled with instinctive
antipathy from a seer like Coleridge.   Literary orthodoxy
of this type leaves no permanent intellectual trace, and
only retains an historical interest as indicating the mental

drift of a community at a particular period. Permanent results, however, were produced by William Emerson's motion for the formation of a club library, which eventually developed into the library of the Boston Athenæum, one of the best upon the continent.

Thus happily and usefully occupied, respected and caressed by society notwithstanding the slenderness of his means, discharging several important public trusts, recognized by the civic authorities as a man of mark, happy in a promising and increasing family, though twice smitten by the loss of young children, William Emerson could write with all sincerity of the sphere in which he found himself, as "an ample and beautiful world in which there has been afforded to me a pleasant lot and much happiness, worthy friends and delightful contemplations." Nor was his a merely fair-weather optimism. When shortly afterwards attacked by an insidious malady, he could write, "To my wife and children, indeed, my continuance upon earth is a matter of moment; as, in the event of my decease, God only knows how they would subsist. And then the education of the latter! But I am not oppressed with this solicitude. Our family, you know, have so long been in the habit of trusting Providence; that none of them ever seriously thought of providing a terrestrial maintenance for themselves and households." Very shortly afterwards (May 12, 1811), he passed away. "Three years before, he had been," says his funeral encomiast, Buckminster, "brought down in an instant, and without any previous warning, to the gates of death, when busily preparing for a public service." This is explained to have been the effect of a profuse hæmorrhage

from the lungs, from the effects of which he never com-
pletely recovered. But the disease of which he died had
no connection with this bleeding, being occasioned by a
tumour which entirely closed the lower orifice of the
stomach. "The town," said Buckminster, a man whose
commendation counts for very much, "has lost a diligent
observer of its youth and their education; the Academy
and Historical Society an associate greatly interested in
their flourishing state; the University an attentive over-
seer. The clergy throughout the country have lost a
hospitable and liberal brother; his family a most careful
and excellent father, husband, and master; and his friends
an honourable and faithful friend."

This warm eulogium was delivered as a part of William Emerson's funeral oration, and subsequently added
to his posthumous and most considerable work, the history
of his own church from 1630 to his own time—a respectable if not brilliant performance, full of curious illustrations of the metamorphosis of Puritan theology, and itself
a conclusive proof of the change which had come over
men's minds. Speaking of the persecutions in which the
old Puritans indulged themselves, he says: "The Bap-
tists still groaned in prisons. The most unrighteous
laws stared them in the face; and the most villainous
conduct was secretly practised to their mischief." Yet
Buckminster attests that Emerson "looked back with
veneration almost unbounded at some of his predeces-
sors." The book was published by his widow in the
December following his death, and probably contributed
something to the relief of her narrow circumstances.
William Emerson must indeed have possessed a large

measure of the faith that walketh not by sight, if he died
with a mind at ease respecting the prospects of his family.
If he depended on his congregation, his confidence was
not vain. The church continued his salary to the widow for
six months, voted her five hundred dollars yearly for seven
years, and allowed her the occupancy of the parsonage
for a year and a half, a term subsequently extended to
three years. Boarders were taken in, most of the household drudgery was performed by Mrs. Emerson herself,
personal friends helped occasionally; the maiden aunt,
Mary Moody Emerson, did her part to the extent of her
scanty means; and so the four boys William (born 1801),
Ralph Waldo (1803), Edward Bliss (1805), Charles Chauncy
(1808), were not only fed and clothed, but liberally educated. Another son, Robert Bulkeley, though an amiable
lad, proved permanently childish and incapable of instruction ; a little girl, born about the time of her father's
death, soon disappeared from the scene. The great
result was not attained without stern self-denial of more
kinds than one, frequent abstinence and occasional priva-
tion. In after-life Miss Emerson concluded a cordial eulogium on her sister with a special reference to her patience
under "the trials of boarders," which she evidently
felt to be no anticlimax : "The most I could say would
not be too much." A friend coming in one day, found the
family without food, and this good aunt, who, let us
trust, *had* dined, "consoling them with stories of heroic
endurance." Ralph and Edward had but one great-coat
between them, no small matter in the winter climate of
New England. The discomforts of this condition were
sufficiently perceptible at the time ; its blessings were

recognized afterwards, when, after a beautiful description of eager, blushing boys comparing the intellectual
treasures amassed in hours snatched from a life of stern
duty and unflinching task-work, Emerson adds :

" What is the hoop that holds them staunch ? It is
the iron band of poverty, of necessity, of austerity, which,
excluding them from the sensual enjoyments which make
other boys too early old, has directed their activity into
safe and right channels, and made them, despite themselves, reverers of the grand, the beautiful, and the good.
Ah, short-sighted students of books, of nature, and of
man ! too happy could they know their advantages, they
pine for freedom from that mild parental yoke ; they
sigh for fine clothes, for riches, for the theatre, and
premature freedom and dissipation which others possess.
Woe to them if their wishes were crowned ! The angels
that dwell with them, and are weaving laurels of life for
their youthful brows, are Toil and Want, and Truth and
Mutual Faith."

It may occur to the reader that if the young Emersons
were staunch, the good aunt who fed the hungry with
tales of the hungrier may have had something to do with
imparting this invaluable quality. So it was ; she was to
Emerson all her life what he, in describing Carlyle's
letters, calls bark and steel and mellow wine. Like most
tonics, she was somewhat tart and astringent ; she idol-
ized her nephews in her own way, but by no means
approved of all their doings or thinkings. She was full
of angularities : a perpetual offender against minor social
proprieties ; orthodox by intellectual conviction, hetero-

dox by native temperament ; "no whistle," said her
nephew, "that every mouth could play on, but a pibroch
from which only a native Highlander could draw music."
Her habitual mode of expressing herself was abrupt and
sibylline ; nor is it clear that she always knew what she
would have. But at rare intervals came some thrilling
oracle; some deliverance only needing epigrammatic point
to have been Emerson's own. "Scorn trifles, lift your
aims," was the burden of all her discourse. "A few
pulsations of created beings," she wrote in 1822, "a few
successions of acts, a few lamps held out in the firmament,
enable us to talk of Time, make epochs with histories,
date the revelations of God to man. It is a goodly name
for our notions of breathing, suffering, enjoying, acting.
We personify it. We call it by every name of dreaming,
fleeting, vapouring imagery. Yet it is nothing. We
exist in eternity. Dissolve the body and the night is
gone, the stars are extinguished, and we measure duration
by the number of our thoughts, by the activity of reason,
the discovery of truths, the acquirement of virtue, the
approach to God. And the grey-haired god throws his
shadows all around, and his slaves catch, now at this,
now at that one ; at the halo he throws around poetry, or
pebbles, or bugs, or bubbles. Sometimes they climb,
sometimes creep into the meanest holes—but they are
all alike in vanishing, like the shadow of a cloud."
Emerson, *mutatis mutandis*, might assuredly have said
with the third Napoleon, *Je suis le neveu de ma tante.*
"She has deserted," he wrote long afterwards, "her
remote village to refresh herself awhile with young faces,
and defend them from parental routine. Perhaps they

will not find in all the colleges so real a benefactor."
The chronicle of his schooldays, complete as regards his
instruction and the routine of study, affords but little
material for constructing a living image of the scholar
himself. Some who have recorded their reminiscences
in late life, evidently speak less of what they saw than of
what they wish they had seen; others candidly admit that
they saw nothing. One fact, however, is both clear in
itself, and a clear proof how entirely in Emerson's as in
most other cases, the child fathered the man. Always
among his school-mates, he was never of them. There
was a certain aloofness which never allowed them to
consider him quite one of themselves ; he was not a
schoolboy, but a boy at school. This peculiar distinction he preserved through his life ; without stiffness or
churlishness, affectation or assumption, he always put
and kept a distance between himself and others, which
rendered his personal influence, apart from his writing
and his oratory, smaller than that of almost any other
great teacher. It is noteworthy that his intimates always
call him *Mr.* Emerson. Enthusiasm never got beyond
the hem of his garment ; and this though the man
was as simple, transparent, and unaffected as if he
had been a great naturalist, instead of a cultivator of
moral science. His isolation was simply the effect of an
unlikeness to others not necessarily indicative of mental
superiority, and so far disadvantageous that in later life
it prevented his exercising that moral control over his
congregation which might have been easily exerted by an
inferior man. The few definite notices that we possess
of him at this early period are mostly indicative of this

involuntary spiritual exclusiveness. "He had then," said
an old schoolfellow to Dr. Holmes, "the same manner and
courtly hesitation in addressing you that you have known
in him since." "He seemed," says the youth he taught
at college, "to dwell apart, as if in a tower, from which
he looked upon everything from a loophole of his own."
Taxed on one occasion with assuming an air of superiority,
he replied with veracious simplicity, "I did not know it,
sir." Such a pretension, had it indeed been advanced,
would have seemed the less justifiable, as he was by no
means a brilliant scholar, or remarkably prominent in his
class. He was indeed, on one occasion, selected to
deliver a poem of his own composition, but only after the
task had been declined by seven of his reputed betters.
"Attended a dissertation of Emerson's in the morning, on
the subject of Ethical Philosophy," writes Josiah Quincy:
"I found it long and dry." And again, "Emerson's vale-
dictory exercise rather poor, and did but little honour to
the class." It was not known that his boyhood had been
fascinated by one of the writers least likely to interest an
average youth, Montaigne; and that he habitually carried
a translation of Pascal's Pensées to church with him.
It is a curious instance of the meeting of extremes that
the most believing of men should have been thus early
attracted to these two great and in different ways typical
sceptics.

Emerson's schooling had commenced before he was
three, and a week ere he attained that ripe age his father
seems half disappointed that "Ralph does not read very
well yet." After another spell of learning under Lawson
Lyon, "a severe teacher," at the age of ten he entered

the Boston Latin School, then or shortly afterwards under an excellent master, Mr. Apthorp Gould. Here he showed a talent for speech-making and rhyming which gained his master's good will, but the only incident of any interest recorded is the whole school turning out to aid in throwing up defences on Noddle Island against an expected visit from the British—then, to the shame of both nations, a hostile fleet. Emerson distinctly remembered the holiday, but could never recollect that the young engineers had done any work. In 1817 he entered Harvard College, under favour of an arrangement resembling a Cambridge sizarship. He was made "President's freshman," or messenger to summon delinquents and announce orders and regulations, which insured him free lodging ; and waiter at Commons, which saved him three-fourths of his board. He also participated in several minor benefactions for poor scholars, and after a while eked out his means still further by giving supplementary lessons to a youth less educated than himself, whose character of him has already been cited, and who, when a distinguished clergyman in after years, gratefully acknowledged his obligation to him— rather as Mentor, however, than as instructor. Emerson's backwardness in mathematics almost brought him into disgrace, and he seems to have evinced no special proficiency except in Greek. The Greek professor, the eloquent Edward Everett, inspired him with enthusiastic admiration ; and the Hellenic bent of his mind was further disclosed by a successful prize essay on Socrates. "Why not Locke, Paley, or Stewart?" asked the President, to whom Cæsar and Pompey were evidently much alike.

Emerson himself could not have told, but he held serenely on his own course, resolute alike in his acceptance of the mental food he found wholesome and his avoidance of that which did not commend itself to his instinct. Like many another active-minded youth in similar circumstances, he indemnified himself for the distastefulness of a large portion of the college course by a wide ranging over general literature. There seems no trace of his study of any modern continental language; but he was deeply versed in Shakespeare and the early English dramatists; and Swift, Addison, and Sterne are named among the authors he introduced to the more intellectual among his classmates. Next to his reserve and the faultless propriety of his conduct, his contemporaries at Harvard seem chiefly impressed with his unusual maturity and such an equipoise of intelligence as might have become a youthful Spinoza, but rarely accompanies the gift of poetry in verse or prose. Nothing about him seemed to indicate the future poet or mystic. There is no trace of the revolt of a Shelley, the suicidal tendencies of a Goethe, or Carlyle's warfare with the Everlasting No: nor did genius ever make its *début* in the world with less passion and crudity, or, it must be added, with less apparent promise. By so much as Emerson was before most men in the balance and discipline of the ordinary faculties of his mind, by so much was he behind most inspired men in the development of the exceptional.

The first indication of deep thought in Emerson's mind is found in a reminiscence of his own, perhaps not wholly accurate in point of date. It professedly

relates to the period immediately succeeding his gra-
duation at Harvard in 1821, when he was assisting his
brother William in a school for ladies which the latter
had established in Boston.　In a speech delivered many
years afterwards, he laments his inability to impart to his
pupils what was chiefly precious to himself.　" My teaching," he says, "was partial and external.　I was at the
very time already writing every night, in my chamber,
my first thoughts on morals and the beautiful laws of
compensation and of individual genius, which to observe
and illustrate have given sweetness to many hours of my
life.　I am afraid no hint of this ever came into the
school, where we clung to the safe and cold details of
languages, geography, arithmetic, and chemistry."　Wordsworth in one of his meditative poems hints his apprehension lest he should unawares " confound the present
feelings with the past," and it must be owned that there
is little in Emerson's correspondence of this period to
intimate the existence of the Essay on Compensation,
even in embryo.　His letters, however, though extant,
have not been fully published ; and a remarkable passage
in one of them (June 19, 1823) shows that he even
then regarded himself as a poet and a worshipper of
Nature.

"I am seeking to put myself on a footing of old
acquaintance with nature, as a poet should ; but the fair
divinity is somewhat shy of my advances, and I confess
I cannot find myself quite as perfectly at home on the
rock and in the wood as my ancient, and I might say
infant, aspirations led me to expect.　My aunt (of whom

I think you have heard before, and who is alone among women) has spent a great part of her life in the country, is an idolater of nature, and counts but a small number who merit the privilege of dwelling among the mountains —the coarse thrifty cit profanes the grove by his presence —and she was anxious that her nephew might hold high and reverential notions regarding it, as the temple where God and the mind are to be studied and adored, and where the fiery soul can begin a premature communication with the other world. When I took my book, therefore, to the woods, I found nature not half poetical, not half visionary enough. There was nothing which the most froward imagination could construe for a moment into a satyr or dryad. No Greek or Roman or even English fantasy could deceive me one instant into the belief of more than met the eye. In short, I found that I had only transplanted into the new place my entire personal identity, and was grievously disappointed. Since I was cured of my air-castles I have fared somewhat better; and a pair of moonlight evenings have screwed up my esteem several pegs higher, by supplying my brain with several bright fragments of thought, and making me dream that mind as well as body respired more freely here."

It is to be observed that the country retreat to which Emerson had repaired when he penned the above lines was by no means a lodge in a vast wilderness, but a wooded corner of the suburban district of Roxbury, picturesque enough, but so near Boston as to have been in our time absorbed by the enlargement of the city.

Mrs. Emerson had there taken up her abode in Canterbury Lane, known also as Light Lane, from the gloom
of the overshadowing trees, and Featherbed Lane, in
compliment to the ruggedness of the roadway. "Poets
succeed better in fiction than in truth." While Emerson
disparaged his sylvan retirement in prose, he was by no
means backward in his claims for it in the following lines,
the first of any importance that he seems to have composed :

> " I am going to my own hearth-stone,
> Burrowed in yon green hills alone,—
> A secret nook in a pleasant land,
> Whose groves the frolic fairies planned ;
> Where arches green the live-long day
> Echo the blackbird's roundelay,
> And vulgar feet have never trod
> A spot that is sacred to thought and God.
>
> Oh when I am safe in my sylvan home,
> I tread on the pride of Greece and Rome ;
> And when I am stretched beneath the pines
> Where the evening star so holy shines,
> I laugh at the lore and the pride of man,
> At the sophist schools and the learned clan ;
> For what are they all in their high conceit,
> When man in the bush with God may meet ? "

These lines, alike in sentiment and cadence, strongly
resemble Pringle's famous " Afar in the Desert," which,
however, was not published until 1828 ; nor can Pringle
have seen them.

The means for Mrs. Emerson's removal to Canterbury
Lane appear to have been supplied by the success of
William's school, which allowed him to proceed to finish

his education in Germany. Waldo, as he was now called by his family and intimates, conducted the school for a year during his brother's absence, and Edward, now a youth of nineteen, established another seminary in Roxbury. By 1825 ~~Waldo's three years of school-keeping~~ had put from two to three thousand dollars into his pocket, and he felt enabled to terminate the parenthesis in his own education by entering the Divinity School at Cambridge, to prepare himself to follow the profession of all those among his ancestors who had been born upon American soil.

CHAPTER II.

THE time when the young schoolmaster thus for a season retrograded into the pupilar condition was one of repose and yet of expectation, pregnant with the germs of great things to come. It was for long afterwards looked back upon with regret as " the era of good feeling." The last prominent statesman of America's heroic age was President; two, more illustrious still, were descending towards the grave in the sight of all; the atmosphere seemed suffused with their departing brightness, and faction stood for the moment abashed by the solemn euthanasia of an age of giants. Meanwhile new issues were silently maturing, new strifes preparing. The carrion instinct of Aaron Burr had truly scented the taint of the coming time when he indicated its coming man in Andrew Jackson, personally honest, but author of that watchword of corruption, "The spoils to the victors." An age was impending of selfish scrambling and shameless manœuvring at home, of offensive hectoring and audacious rapacity abroad; an age which might have seemed permitted to show to what a depth a free and enlightened people can descend, if it had not even more impressively demonstrated from what a depth such a people can recover itself. That America did recover was due in no small manner to her good fortune in preserving a moral and intellectual aristocracy, whose hereditary descent from the very flower of seventeenth-century England had not been lost in the turbid torrent of miscellaneous immigration. No less happy was it that, thanks to federal sovereignty and local institutions, this aristocratic element was not, like so many aristocracies, imbecile or effete, but retained a healthy interest in public life, and was neither too timid nor too superfine to face a political issue and fight a stiff election. No man was to contribute more to keep New England in essentials what the Pilgrim Fathers had made it, than the unnoticed student of a system of theology which was ruthlessly dissolving the mere externalities of the Pilgrim Fathers' creed. To lift Unitarianism out of sectarianism, to transform an originally rationalistic mode of thought into a mystic and transcendental one, to kill it as theology and bid it live as literature, were tasks reserved for the young student which would have dismayed him could he have caught one dimmest glimpse of them as he entered the Cambridge Divinity School.

In choosing the Church as his profession, Emerson followed the path which seemed marked for one in whose veins ran so much clerical blood, but at the same time he obeyed his own conviction of what was best. He had formed a sound estimate of his powers, and believed that in the course he was following he should do them justice. He fancied, indeed, that " his abilities were below his ambition ;" but this might well be, since his aspiration, though unambitious of worldly distinction, contemplated great results in the intellectual world ; *inmensum infinitum-*

que aliquid. He fully recognized that his logical faculty compared unfavourably with his imagination, but he remarked with justice that this was no reason why he should abstain from theology, " for the highest species of reasoning upon divine subjects is rather the fruit of a sort of moral imagination than of the reasoning machines, such as Locke and Clarke and David Hume." He proceeds to instance Channing's Dudleian lecture as his model, and his admiration did not misguide him. There is not, perhaps, in the whole arena of theological literature such another instance of clear calm sense exalted to the highest eloquence by devoutness of spirit and moral enthusiasm as is afforded by the discourses of Channing. Whatever is best in the seventeenth and the eighteenth century pulpit seems united in this ornament of the nineteenth : but out of the pulpit the charm of Channing's elo-quence, if not dispelled, lost much of its fascination. The fervent, faultless man of God whose heroic attitude and serene eloquence could fire multitudes and quell mobs seemed to have little faculty for dealing with his fellow men face to face. An atmosphere of reserve environed him ; he gave forth more light than heat. Emerson's personal resort to him ended in disappoint-ment ; he was hardly capable, the younger man thought, of taking another person's point of view, or of com-municating himself freely in private conversation. " He does not converse," said George Combe, " but delivers an essay, and waits patiently to hear an essay in return." His peculiar secret of exalting morality into religion by enthusiasm for the right and good was Emerson's already by natural endowment ; so that the latter could not feel that he had much to learn from him, nor did he find another guide. He wrote indeed freely of his perplexities to his aunt Mary, but his interrogations seem rather soliloquies than dialogues. After all, his difficulties were no more than must naturally occur to every thoughtful person. He was not blind to the strong points of the old Puritan theology. "Presbyterianism and Calvinism make Christianity a more real and tangible system, and give it some novelties which were worth unfolding to the ignorance of men." But he felt no disposition to accept the assumptions on which it was based. "That the administration of eternity is fickle, that the God of revelation hath seen cause to repent and botch up the ordinances of the God of Nature, I hold it not irreverent but impious in us to assume." He was not too well satisfied with the average standard of devotional fervour in the Unitarian Church ; but many had transcended it, and why not he ? " I know that there are in my vicinity clergymen who are not merely literary or philosophical." He was not, therefore, like John Sterling, erring from precipitancy, when he deliberately adopted the clerical profession : indeed, like almost all the acts of his singularly symmetrical and harmonious life, the step was decidedly the wisest that he could have taken at the time.

Seldom, however, has neophyte been more buffeted by accident and fatality than Emerson. He had scarcely been a month at the Cambridge Divinity School ere his overtasked eyes failed him, and general debility drove him to the country, " to try the experiment of hard work for the benefit of health." It profited him; but more than a

year elapsed ere he returned to Cambridge. In the
interim he had for a short time taken charge of a school
at Chelmsford, and afterwards of that established at Roxbury by his brother Edward, the genius, it was then
deemed, of the family, who had overtasked his strength,
and been driven to try a voyage to the Mediterranean.
A pupil of Emerson's at the Chelmsford School remembers
his grave and quiet, yet engaging demeanour, the subjection in which he could keep the boys by a look or a
tone, a peculiar expression in his eyes, as if he saw things
invisible to others. Mr. John Holmes, the brother of
Oliver Wendell Holmes, records his undoubting calmness
of manner, the sternness of his very infrequent rebukes, his
kindliness in explaining or advising. " Every inch a king
in his dominicn. Looking back, he seems to me rather
like a captive philosopher set to tending flocks." " He
was not," says another witness, " especially successful as a
teacher. He was studying for the ministry, and his heart
was centred in his studies. Still, everything went along
with the utmost smoothness." While he was at Chelmsford an incident occurred which must have strengthened
his resolution to be a minister, had it needed strengthen-
ing. This was the aberration of his brother William,
who had gone to study theology in Germany, and there
imbibed doubts which withheld him from the Church.
Foreseeing the pain which this would occasion his mother,
he had sought counsel from Goethe, who received him
sympathetically, and, true to his own preference for the concrete over the abstract, recommended him rather to conceal
his scruples than grieve his kindred. Conscience, however, had the mastery in William's mind, and he forsook

theology for law, rising ultimately to the judicial bench. Some congregation lost something, for, according to his cousin George, William Emerson had the sweetest voice ever heard. Upon his return he visited Waldo at Chelmsford to discuss the matter with him. "I was very sad," says Emerson, "for I knew how it would grieve my mother, and it did." The more reason, then, that he himself should adhere to the path she had wished, and he had chosen.

Though unable to join the regular class at Cambridge, Emerson had occasionally attended lectures, and the authorities, convinced of his worth and seriousness, and perhaps recognizing his hereditary claim to ordination, were content to dispense with any considerable acquaintance with technical divinity. If they had examined him, he said afterwards, his licence would assuredly have been refused. "Approbated to preach" by the Middlesex Association of Ministers on October 10, 1826, he delivered his first discourse at Waltham five days afterwards. The subject was suggested by the remark of a labourer with whom he had worked when striving to fortify his constitution by rustic toil in the preceding year—"a Methodist, who, though ignorant and rude, had some deep thoughts. He said to me that men were always praying, and that all prayers were granted. I meditated much on this saying, and wrote my first sermon therefrom; of which the divisions were (1) Men are always praying; (2) All their prayers are granted; (3) We must beware, then, what we ask." Emerson could hardly have begun his career as a public teacher more characteristically than by the unfolding of so deep a truth so sheathed in apparent

paradox : nor was it less like himself to waive at the very
outset his own academical claims in favour of the simple
wisdom of one " taught of the Spirit."

A month later, shortly after his brother Edward's
return from Europe, in improved health, but with a
burden of debt contracted to defray the expenses of his
tour, which preyed upon his sensitive conscience, and
eventually broke him down, Emerson was driven south
by a recurrence of his chest complaint. After a short
stay at Charleston, he journeyed on to St. Augustine, in
Florida, but recently acquired by the United States, and
still far more Spanish than Anglo-American. " An
ancient, fortified, dilapidated sand-bank of a town,"
whose population of twelve hundred was unequally
divided between Americans fulfilling their manifest
destiny as office-holders, and Spanish families· with
retinues of blacks. " The Americans live on their
offices ; the Spaniards keep billiard tables ; or, if not,
they send their negroes to the mud to bring oysters, or
to the shore to bring fish, and the rest of the time fiddle,
mask, and dance. It was reported in the morning that
a man was at work in the public square, and all our
family turned out to see him. I stroll on the sea-beach,
and drive a green orange over the sand with a stick." He
could not have been better employed. Health came
back gradually in the mild air, and his mental development was assisted by some practical insight into the
system of slavery, and by acquaintance with the first
foreigner he had known intimately, a man of a different
type to any he had yet encountered. This was no other
than Achille Murat, son of King Joachim and nephew

of Napoleon, at that time a planter at Tallahassee. "A philosopher, a scholar, a man of the world; very sceptical, but very candid, and an ardent lover of truth." Emerson accompanied him to his plantation, and they were fellow passengers on ship-board back to Charleston. He reached home in June, stopping and preaching on the way at Charleston, Washington, Philadelphia, and New York. The abstraction from purely professional duties and interests had certainly benefited him. His aspirations had become more varied, his tastes more versatile; he felt at times, he tells his aunt, as though he might become a novelist or a poet; he even experienced spasmodic yearnings to be a painter. These growth-pains of genius did not perturb his demeanour; he was still regarded as a staid young man, rather pedantically exact in keeping his diary, and far less promising than his brilliant brother Edward. His originality was mainly manifested in the decision of his ethics. He preached independence. "Owe no conformity to custom," he said, "against your private judgment." "Have no regard to the influence of your example, but act always from the simplest motive." But while thus asserting his right to disregard social conventions if he saw fit, he apparently felt no call to quarrel with them. He comported himself like other young ministers; he was neither a Spiritualist nor a Free Lover, nor even a vegetarian. His one eccentricity could be indulged without attracting attention. " It is a peculiarity of humour in me, my strong propensity for strolling. I deliberately shut up my books in a cloudy July noon, put on my old clothes and old hat, and slink away to the whortleberry bushes, and slip with the greatest satisfaction into a little cow-path, where I am sure I can defy observation. This point gained, I solace myself for hours with picking blueberries and other trash of the woods, far from fame behind the birch trees. I seldom enjoy hours as I do these. I remember them in winter; I expect them in spring. I do not know a creature that I think has the same humour, or would think it respectable." The impressions thus imbibed were to be given back in due season. Emerson's best writings are the breathings of a soul saturated with sylvan influences.

For nearly a year Emerson continued a student at Divinity Hall, "his health the same stupid riddle that it always had been," "treading on eggs to strengthen his constitution," "lingering on system, writing something less than a sermon a month." The happy consequence was that in April, 1828, he reports himself as "looking less like a monument and more like a man." In what may be termed his moral regimen, he seems, as in most things, to have been a model. He had nothing of the peevishness of the invalid. "I court laughing persons, and after a merry or only a gossiping hour, when the talk has been mere soap-bubbles, I have lost all sense of the mouse in my chest, am at ease, and can take my pen or book." He adds that he has just refused the third "Church Applicant" wanting him to preach as a candidate.

The easy stream of his life was soon to be ruffled by a painful, almost a tragic event. Waldo, the dutiful youth who followed the career desired by his mother, who had never been overtaken in a fault or had given a moment's uneasiness to those who loved him, save from the weakness of his health, was in that day regarded rather as the example than the hope of his family.. He had not, like William, strayed even beyond the ample limits of Unitarian orthodoxy ; nor had he exhibited the versatility, nigh akin to instability, of his brilliant brother Edward. But the family pride and hope were concentrated on the latter. "Born for success," writes Waldo,

> " He seemed,
> With grace to win, with heart to hold,
> With shining gifts that took all eyes,
> With budding power in college halls,
> As pledged in coming days to forge
> Weapons to guard the State, or scourge
> Tyrants despite their guards or walls."

This glowing estimate was confirmed by the judgment of impartial observers. "There was no presage," writes Dr. Hedge, "of Emerson's future greatness. His promise seemed faint in comparison with the wondrous brilliancy of his younger brother, Edward Bliss Emerson, whose immense expectation was doomed never to be fulfilled." "Refinement of thought and selectness in the use of language," were indeed notable in Waldo, but only so far as "to give promise of an interesting preacher to cultivated hearers." But Edward Emerson's college career had been as brilliant as Waldo's had been the reverse. He appeared marked for a leader of men, and exerted a magnetic spell, still potent after sixty years with the few who remember him. " Oh what a teacher Edward Bliss

Emerson was !" exclaims Mr. Harrington. "A gift of God to those he taught. A model of manly beauty of the highest type in form and feature. Immaculate purity of soul, intellectual greatness, exquisite refinement of feeling and tenderest sensibility, were all engaged in limning its wonderful attractions. Had the lives of Edward and Charles been spared beyond early manhood, the Emerson name would have been still more often spoken." This treasure had been confided to an earthen vessel. Edward's constitution was as delicate as Waldo's, but while the latter was screened by a pensive temperament, inasmuch that, as he said himself, "he could mend his shell with pearl," Edward's genius summoned him to external activity. The strain was too great for him. His health, as has been seen, had already broken down in school-keeping. Returning from Europe, as he fondly deemed with renovated strength, he had consecrated himself with the devotion of a Walter Scott to the task of freeing himself from his pecuniary obligations. In pursuance of this end he had tried one employment after another without success, and the fret of failure at length wore out not only the body, but the mind. In June, 1828, Emerson was hastily summoned to his brother, who "had fainting fits and delirium, and had been strangely affected in his mind for a fortnight." A delusive improvement was succeeded by a state of violent derangement. "There he lay—Edward, the admired, learned, eloquent, strong boy—a maniac." The paroxysm was temporary. Edward recovered and retained his reason, but his health never returned. His wing was broken ; he sought the West Indies, and there, during the brief respite thus snatched from the grave, the youth who might have been the foremost citizen of his state, lived obscurely as a commercial clerk. Pondering over this tragedy, Emerson became almost thankful for his own defects, which he came to regard as ballast. "My manner," he says, with the exaggeration of self-reproach, "is sluggish, my speech sometimes flippant, sometimes embarrassed and ragged; my actions (if I may say so) are of a passive kind. My brother lived and acted with preternatural energy." Hence Emerson arrived at the comfortable conclusion that, having so little mind to lose, he need not be afraid of losing any. His insignificance was to protect him. "Do you think," said the old Irish retainer to the new-comers, "that the Banshee would wail for the likes of *ye?*"

Prosperity and love joined hands to lift him from this depression. If he thought meanly of himself, others, it was clear, did not. In the autumn of 1828, the pulpit of the Second Church, one of the most important in Boston, seemed likely to be vacant by the illness of Henry Ware. Emerson was invited to fill it during the pastor's illness: but a report got abroad that Mr. Ware, upon his recovery, would accept a professorship at Cambridge, and Emerson, with refined sensitiveness, scrupled at the advantage which occupation of the pulpit would have given him over other candidates. He thought all should start fair. "If I am settled," he said, "I choose it should not be because I have kept a better man from being heard." Mr. Ware did not resign, but accepted a colleague, and early in 1829 Emerson was elected by seventy-four out of seventy-nine votes. Within a

few weeks Ware found it necessary to seek health in
Europe, and Emerson became sole incumbent. It was
no doubt exceedingly welcome to him to have been spared
the usual ordeal of competitive oratory : and another
circumstance had probably weight in determining him
to accept a position for which he had previously manifested but little eagerness. On December 24, 1828, he
informed his brother William that he had been for a week
engaged to Ellen Tucker, a young lady of seventeen,
daughter of a deceased Boston merchant, living at
Concord with her mother and stepfather.   He had been
smitten with her a year before, but "thought I had got
over my blushes and my wishes."   "I saw Ellen at once,"
he wrote afterwards, "in all her beauty, and she never
disappointed me except in her death."   Ellen Emerson,
as she became in September, 1829, faded so quickly out
of life and all memories but her husband's, that little
seems to be known of her beyond her remarkable beauty,
her fatal delicacy of constitution, and her buoyant spirit.
Within a month of her engagement she made Emerson
miserable by spitting blood. The deceptive malady, as
usual, left much apparent ground for hope. We have
seen that it did not prevent their union eight months
afterwards.   In February he wrote : "Ellen is mending
day by day. 'Twould take more time than I can spare
to tell how excellent a piece of work she is. She trifles so
much with all her ails, and loses no jot of spirits, that we
talk gravely only when asunder." She wrote verse ; one
of her little poems, preserved in "The Dial," seems to
imply acquaintance with Goethe : and to her, about this
time, were addressed these charming verses :

" Thine eyes still shined for me, though far
    I lonely roved the land or sea :
As I behold yon evening star,
    Which yet beholds not me.

This morn I climbed the misty hill,
    And roamed the pastures through :
How danced thy form before my path,
    Amid the deep-eyed dew !

When the redbird spread his sable wing,
    And showed his side of flame ;
When the rosebud ripened to the rose,
    In both I read thy name."

It seems almost needful to the full exhibition of the
contrast between Emerson and his great compeer and
complement beyond the Atlantic, that he should have
deliberately chosen the calling which Carlyle as deliberately rejected. Emerson was fit and knew himself fit for
the office of teacher by public speech : Carlyle must have
recognized his incapacity for it even independently of the
restraints of creed and confession which formed his os-
tensible reason for declining it. He denounced his own
lecturing as "a mixture of prophecy and play acting ; "
and had the Kirk of Scotland been as liberal as the Unitarian Church of New England he would soon have
chafed at the indispensable accompaniments of the
pastoral office. To Emerson's apprehension, on the other
hand, ministerial duty presented nothing distasteful : he
would willingly have spent his life in the service of a congregation, however humble, could he but have had liberty
always to tell them the highest thing he knew, and to con-
form his practice in all respects with his ideal. The
right and duty of free inquiry, sometimes as passionately

asserted as though they needed demonstration, appeared
to him self-evident : but at the outset of his ministerial
career he could not know that he would be carried beyond
the latitude accorded by the most tolerant of churches;
ʰ] nor, even in this case, could he foresee that his flock
would refuse to follow him "to fresh woods and pastures
new." He began, therefore, with perfect sincerity, in a
thoroughly hopeful spirit, holding out, in the manifesto
which in compliance with usage he addressed to his congregation in his first sermons, no promise of any novelty
except the freer use of familiar language and homely illustration. " I said to myself," he tells his aunt, " that if
men would avoid that general language and general
manner in which they strive to hide all that is peculiar, every man would be interesting." The written
record of his ministry lies before his literary executor,
Mr. Cabot, in one hundred and seventy-one manuscript
sermons. In deference to his own wish they are withheld from the press, but Mr. Cabot gives a general
account of their characteristics. According to this they
are mainly remarkable for the absence of any special
originality of thought or phrase. There is no endeavour
after the rhetorical effectiveness then in vogue; and all
is clear, earnest, and direct. Whether the logical sequence of thought is better observed than in the Essays,
Mr. Cabot does not tell us. As the preacher's mind
ripened his individuality became more distinct, but so
long as he occupied the pulpit his ideas were presented
in Scriptural language, as if they belonged to the body of
accepted doctrine. A specimen of this method of reading
new truth out of, and into, an old text, is afforded by the

reminiscence of a hearer who heard Emerson preach on
"What is a man profited if he gain the whole world and
lose his own soul?" The main emphasis was on the
word "own," and the general theme was that to every
man the great end of existence was the preservation and
culture of his individual mind and character. One can
understand from this the remark of another hearer : "In
looking back on his preaching I find he has impressed
truths to which I always assented, in such a manner as to
make them appear new, like a clearer revelation." His
popularity, if not showy, was substantial ; he belonged to
public bodies and took part in public affairs; though
no politician, he opened his church to the first movers in
the anti-slavery agitation ; and seemed in a fair way to
prove what to many so-called liberals seems doubtful,
that there is no incompatibility between independent
thought and the public ministrations of religion. If his
discourse could not impress the world like Carlyle's, as a
sudden vent for impassioned feelings, the silent accumu-
lation of many years of fierce inward conflict, he could
hold religion up to men as a serene lamp lit at the tran-
quil but intense flame which burned in his own bosom.
He could and did avoid the great stumbling-block of the
teacher by the touch of genius which redeems familiar
truth from platitude and commonplace, and, according
to a happy definition, presents religion not merely as
morality, but as morality touched with emotion. In the
duties of pastoral visitation he seems to have been less
efficient ; and here indeed it is easy to conceive that nice
refinement and respect for the sacredness of other men's
convictions may sometimes prove a disqualification, and

that obtrusiveness may be a condition of success. "Young man," said a spiritual patient, scandalized at not being treated *secundum artem*, "if you don't know your business, you had better go home." It is characteristic of his deep humanity, and his aversion to fuss and commonplace, that he appeared to least advantage at a funeral. A professional observer, a sexton, remarked that on such occasions "he did not seem to be at ease at all. To tell the truth, in my opinion, that young man was not born to be a minister." Emerson was soon to feel the need of such qualifications as ministers of less refined but stronger mould bring to bear upon their congregations : but, though defeat for lack of them was bitter, such victory as they could have given would not have been valued by him.

Ere the coming of that day, however, Emerson had to bear a far heavier calamity. His marriage, obedient to the dictates of affection, had set at nought those of physical prudence. Even in the first flush of triumphant love he had been conscious of the coming shadow. "Will God," he had written, "make me an exception to the common order of his dealings, which equalises destinies ? I cannot find in the world any antidote, any bulwark against this fear like this, the frank acknowledgment of unbounded dependence. If I am called, after the way of my race, to pay a fatal tax for my good, I may appeal to the sentiment of collected anticipation with which I saw the tide turn and the winds blow softly from the favouring west." His forebodings were speedily fulfilled. In the first winter of their marriage it was necessary to take Ellen to the south, and as he was meditating a second journey the plan was frustrated by her rapid decline, terminating in death in February, 1831. She had been to him "a bright revelation of the best nature of woman." Reserved as he was in the expression of personal emotion, his diary is long afterwards chequered with cries of sorrow in prose and verse ; and until his departure for Europe he daily sought her grave.

The year following his bereavement (1832) was to see Emerson widowed also of his spiritual bride, his church. It was not a divorce on account of incompatibility. There is nothing to show that he felt the least uneasiness in the clerical habit, of which indeed he did not divest himself for some time afterwards. But it was a necessary condition of his ministry that he should be at liberty to follow his own highest conceptions ; if these clashed with the requirements of his congregation, their connection could no longer endure. The cause of difference was characteristic of his independence : it related to a rite which nine-tenths of those who felt with him would have tolerated as harmless. Religious persons may from one point of view be distinguished according as they do or do not feel the need of external ceremonies in worship. To some, painting, music, gorgeous vestments, seem the appropriate apparel of religion ; to others, they are an impertinence, almost an offence. Which temper represents the higher conception need not be discussed here ; but as a matter of fact it is certain that while the ancient religions blazed with ritual splendour, the founders of more spiritual creeds have always striven to reduce this to a minimum, and none more so than the Founder of Christianity. The only two rites to

which he gave his sanction might be deemed to represent
the *ne plus ultra* of ceremonial simplicity; but a germ
remained, prolific in strange growths. No church, probably, was less obnoxious to sacramentalism than
Emerson's; but he could not be content so long as the
pure simplicity of worship was, in his view, desecrated by
any material contact. He easily persuaded himself that
the Lord's Supper had not been designed as a permanent
institution; but let the contrary be conceded, and he was
still ready to add, "If I believed that it was I should not
adopt it. I should choose other ways which, as more
effectual upon me, he would approve more. For I choose
that my remembrances of him should be pleasing, affect-
ing, religious. I will love him as a glorified friend, after
the free way of friendship, and not pay him a stiff sign
of respect, as men do to them whom they fear." He
went on to protest that he was not "so foolish as to declaim against forms. Forms are as essential as bodies;
but to exalt particular forms, to adhere to one form a
moment after it is outgrown, is unreasonable, and it is
alien to the spirit of Christ." Here was the question in
a nut-shell, as respected Emerson's connection with his
congregation. He had outgrown the form, or thought he
had, but had they? It quickly appeared that his scruples
were unintelligible to them. It was equally apparent
that they no more wished him to go than he wished to be
gone. Compromises were suggested, but proved imprac-
ticable. He would have remained if the material elements could have been dispensed with, and the service
made purely commemorative. They would have let him
deal with the symbols as he pleased, provided that they

were retained.. He retreated into the country to ponder
over the matter, while rumours of his mental derangement went abroad. These he did not condescend to
refute : but to his friends, urging him not to stickle over-
much for points of form, he replied that his punctilious-
ness was rather for his people than himself. " I cannot
go habitually to an institution which they esteem holiest
with indifference or dislike." " It is my desire," he said,
in the address in which he announced his resignation
(Sept. 9th) "to do nothing which I cannot do with my
whole heart. Having said this, I have said all. I
have no hostility to this institution ; I am only stating
my want of sympathy with it. I am content that it
stand to the end of the world, if it please men and please
Heaven, and I shall rejoice in all the good it produces."
The dignity of this farewell is not exempt from a certain
soreness. Emerson was, indeed, pained and mortified ;
he had hoped to have carried his people with him, and
though still considering himself as a clergyman, felt
thenceforward something of "a grudge against preaching." He could not conceal from himself that the pastoral career to which everything had seemed to invite him
had been a failure : nor could it then be seen what a
necessary and invaluable stage it had been in his own
development. " I look back," he said in his farewell
letter of Dec. 22nd, " with a painful sense of weakness to
the little service I have been able to render after so much
expectation on my part." But the springs of hope and
energy were not destroyed. " Shall I pester you," he
wrote to his brother William, " with half the projects.
that sprout and bloom in my head, of action, literature,

philosophy?" Action, however, imperatively requires health, which cannot well be spared even by literature and philosophy. Emerson's vitality was at the time low; he had never got over his domestic sorrow; he could not himself quite resist a feeling of discouragement, and seemed to those about him to have mistaken his vocation. "When a man would be a reformer he needs to be strong," wrote his more pugnacious brother Charles. "The disappointment grows upon me as I go Sunday after Sunday and hear ordinary preachers, and remember what a torch of kindling eloquence has been snuffed out in such an insignificant fashion." Emerson determined on a vigorous step. He had thought of seeking repose and change with his brother Edward in the West Indies, "but in a few hours the dream changed into a purpureal vision of Naples and Italy." He wrote a final letter of affectionate farewell to his people, and in a fortunate hour, December 25, 1832, embarked in the brig *Jasper*, bound with a cargo of West Indian produce for Malta, where she arrived on the 2nd of February.

CHAPTER III.

EMERSON'S *Lehrjahre* were now over, and his brief *Wanderjahr* was about to begin. He had passed through the only episode in his life which in the least savoured of spiritual crisis. Even this character, in so far as it belonged at all to his resignation of his charge, was purely accidental and external. It need not have happened but for others; his own development had never been arrested or diverted; he had travelled quietly on his original line. He had ever followed wisdom as one follows an art or science: it was no more a requisite for him "to adore what he had burned, and to burn what he had adored," than for the young artist at a given period of his career to burn his pencils, or for the young astronomer to shatter his telescope. If he had been taxed with the lack of such experience as befell Paul on the road to Damascus, he might have replied with Paul on another occasion, "I was born free." He had not, like Shelley, prematurely taken up ground which he found himself unable to maintain; nor had he, like Newman, surrendered himself to a current whose inevitable direction he long mistook. He needed no conversion, only a new atmosphere to foster such tendencies of his mind as had failed to receive due nutriment at home.

Yet, as every nature craves its opposite and complement, one object of the serene optimist's travel was to seek the modern representative of Paul, Luther, and Wesley, the victorious but sorely scarred antagonist of the " Everlasting No "—Thomas Carlyle, whose early writings, the writer's name as yet unknown, Emerson had been the first American to receive as a revelation.

The hero, unless also a martyr, generally appears upon the scene at the right time. Europe was just in the state in which an intellectually inquisitive visitor would have desired to find her. Experiments were being tried everywhere, including the experiment of standing still. Peace reigned in every European land, save for one local civil war, but the existing political order was undermined everywhere except in England and Russia, and hostile tendencies had never clashed more fiercely in the world of thought. Liberalism was the ruling creed in theory, even among the statesmen who resisted it in practice; but a formidable ré-action was already visible in the intellectual sphere. Newman was striving to reconcile the old Church with Anglicanism, Lamennais with socialism. Mediæval architecture was coming into fashion; the artistic and literary ideals of the preceding century were falling into disrepute. The Goths of the Romantic school had for the time overwhelmed the traditional classicalism of the Latin nations. Scott reigned in all European literatures; Byron was still a great power; the seed sown by Shelley and Keats was beginning to come up, though their names, like those of Wordsworth and Coleridge, were as yet only heard in England and America. Hegel had just repeated the feat and the

failure of Jonathan Edwards in constructing a system which
none could refute and few could receive. Goethe had done
more for European thought by impregnating it with those
germs of an evolutionary doctrine which afforded a battle-
ground to the savants of Paris, while Lyell gave the idea
of geological uniformity scientific shape in England, and
Darwin yet geologized in South America. Steam was
just above the horizon, and electricity just below it.
On the whole, till the leadings of Providence became
more evident, the intellectual condition of society must
have appeared splendidly anarchical; an impression
which could but be confirmed by the extraordinary
mortality which had recently taken place among the
sovereigns of thought. "*Les dieux s'en vont,*" said Heine.
Within a year death had removed Goethe, Scott, Hegel,
Bentham, and Cuvier. Chateaubriand had retired from
active life, and Coleridge was shortly to retire from the
world. A great void was thus made for the Titanic
Hugos and Carlyles of the age, and its as yet obscure
Comtes and Emersons.

In the first letter he wrote home from Europe, Emerson described the purpose of his journey as being "to
find new affinities between me and my fellow men." Art
and scenery were subordinate objects. " I collected," he
said afterwards, "neither cameo, nor painting, nor
medallion; but I valued much, as I went on, the growing
pictures which the ages had painted and I reverently
surveyed." When, having crossed from Malta into Sicily,
he finds himself at Syracuse, he is disappointed that
"there was scarce anything that speaks of Hiero, or
Timoleon, or Dion. Yet I am glad to be where they

have been, and to hear the bees, and pick beautiful wild
flowers only three or four miles from the fountain Cyane.'
" How evanescent and superficial," he exclaims when in
Rome, " is most of that emotion which names and
places, which art or magnificence, can awaken! It
yields in me to the interest which the most ordinary
companion inspires." Yet he admired works of art
though reversing the traveller's ordinary practice by
displaying more discrimination than enthusiasm. The
churches struck him particularly, and he was impressed
with the value of the æsthetic element in religion,
of which he had had no previous experience. He
was equally surprised that the Americans who had
entered European churches should submit to such mean
edifices at home; and that Italians on their side should
be unable to " devise ceremonies in as good and manly
taste as their churches and pictures and music." The
sum total of his impressions, however, came to much the
same as he afterwards delivered in his suggestive but
defective Essay on Art : " Painting seems to be to
the eye what dancing is to the limbs. When that has
educated the frame to self-possession, to nimbleness, to
grace, the steps of the dancing-master are better forgotten." The one thing he really valued abroad was to
be able " to recognize the same man under a thousand
masks, and to hear the same commandment spoken to
me in Italian I was wont to hear in English. My greatest
want is that I never meet with men who are great or
interesting." The first exception he mentions is Landor,
whom he sought out with an instinct not granted to
many Englishmen of that day. Emerson found him

"living in a cloud of pictures at his Villa Gherardesca," and though he could not deem Landor's real conversation equal to his imaginary ones, he was able to say "He has a wonderful brain, despotic, violent, inexhaustible, meant for a soldier, by chance converted to letters." He afterwards, before reaching England, pronounces Landor one of the two men in Europe to whom he had been able to say something in earnest. This was written in Paris, where he had arrived on June 20th, after a flying visit to Venice, "a city for beavers," and Geneva, where he only visited Voltaire's château under protest. New England thought had travelled a long way since Franklin brought his grandson to be blessed by the Patriarch of Ferney. Paris was pronounced by Emerson "a loud modern New York of a place," but, at the same time, "the most hospitable of cities." He was in London by July 21st, meeting Mill, whom he does not seem to have appreciated, and Bowring, who showed him over the house of Jeremy Bentham. A more memorable interview, "though rather a spectacle than a conversation" ("I was glad," says Sir Henry Taylor, "to *show* him to Stephen"), was that with Coleridge, "a short, thick old man, with bright blue eyes and fine clear complexion, leaning upon his cane." Coleridge's conversation was so far that of a poet that its course obeyed the impulse of any casual incident or allusion. The sight of a militiaman is recorded to have brought him to the fall of Napoleon by way of the Peninsular War, and now the aspect of a Unitarian minister led him to declaim against Unitarianism, of whose later development he cannot have known much if he really took Channing for a follower of Priestley. One of his remarks,

however, was worthy to have found its way into "Table-
Talk." "I have known ten persons who loved the good
for one person who loved the true; but it is a far greater
virtue to love the true for itself alone, than to love the
good for itself alone."

Immediately after his interview with Coleridge Emerson repaired to Scotland, passing, as an allusion in
"Nature" shows, by way of York. He was now to meet
one who fully complied with Coleridge's standard, if indeed Emerson was right, as assuredly he was, in finding the
secret of Carlyle's superiority "in his commanding sense of
justice, and incessant demand for sincerity." When
(Aug. 26th) he alighted at Craigenputtock and met
Carlyle, whose address he had the greatest difficulty in
discovering, he "found him one of the most simple and
frank of men, and became acquainted with him at once.
We walked over several miles of hills, and talked upon
all the great questions that interest us most." "That
man," Carlyle said to Lord Houghton, "came to see me;
I don't know what brought him, and we kept him one
night, and then he left us. I saw him go up the hill. I
didn't go with him to see him descend. I preferred to
watch him mount and vanish like an angel." Most fortunate it was for them both that their meeting lasted so
long and no longer, that there was time to disclose the
general unity of spirit and identity of aspiration, and not
time enough for the discovery of the utter antithesis of
temperament, and the innumerable discrepancies in
points of detail. They parted, each believing the
other intellectually much nearer than he really was: and
this belief fostered a sympathy which, by the time that

their differences became undeniably manifest, had grown too strong and habitual to be seriously disturbed by them. Carlyle's genius, in fact, had not then fully received its epic and dramatic bent; and he was still much under the influence of metaphysical ideas borrowed from Germany. The full report of their conversation is not preserved, but if in comparing notes they began with their fundamental beliefs, they would travel far before they arrived at their points of disagreement. Each was a Pantheist, seeing in the universe a living organism, not something made by an external craftsman. Each was a Transcendentalist, believing in necessary ideas independent of experience. Each passionately asserted a Law of Right, independent of utility or expediency. By the time that these points of contact had been thoroughly established, it may have been in every sense time for Emerson to go. Some genuine Carlyleana came out notwithstanding. Mirabeau *should* be a hero. Gibbon was the splendid bridge from the old world to the new. The great booksellers had paid such incredible sums for puffery that they were all on the verge of bankruptcy. Carlyle had matched his wits against his pig's, with humiliating results. An unfinished bit of road was "the grave of the last sixpence." Not the least remarkable feature in the interview was the perfectly equal footing of him whose genius was acknowledged at least by his visitor, and the thinker as yet entirely unknown to fame. Emerson had made a long pilgrimage to see Carlyle. Carlyle could not have been expected to go a step out of his way to see Emerson. It might have seemed inevitable that they should meet as disciple and master, but it was not so. They associated without embarrassment on the one side, or assumption on the other, each feeling the essential point to be not what a man achieved, but what he was.

Emerson's impressions of Carlyle were first communicated to a young Scotchman, destined to eminence as a journalist and a man of letters, but who will perhaps be even longer remembered as the first European who recognized a light of the age in the American stranger. Emerson had come to Edinburgh with an introduction from Bowring to Dr. John Gairdner, a friend of Mr. Alexander Ireland, " who, luckily for me," says Mr. Ireland, " was so much engaged in professional duties that he was unable to spare a few hours to do the honours of the Scottish metropolis," so his bishopric was taken by another, "and thus I became," says Mr. Ireland, " an entertainer of angels unawares." Never before had Mr. Ireland " met with any one of so fine and varied a culture, and with such frank sincerity of speech. A refined and delicate courtesy, a kind of mental hospitality, so to speak—the like of which, or anything approaching to which, I have never encountered—seemed to be a part of his very nature, and inseparable from his daily walk and conversation." The impression was deepened when, on August 18th, Mr. Ireland heard him preach in the Unitarian church, and remarked the effect produced notwithstanding the absence of all oratorical effort. "Not long before this I had listened to a wonderful sermon by Dr. Chalmers, whose force and energy and vehement eloquence carried for the moment all before them. But I must confess that the pregnant thoughts and serene self-possession of the young Boston minister had a greater charm for me than all the rhetorical splendours of Chalmers." In the intervals of sight-seeing Emerson discoursed of life and literature, of Coleridge and Goethe, Landor and Channing and Montaigne ; and Mr. Ireland's enthusiasm found vent in memoranda, less of what he had heard than of the anticipations for Emerson's future with which Emerson's discourse had inspired him. " They might at that time have sounded unduly inflated, but his subsequent career may be said to have rendered them almost tame and inadequate." Emerson on his part was so interested in his new friend as to send him accounts—most interesting from their freshness and unpremeditation—of his visits to Carlyle and Wordsworth, both of whom he sought on his way to Liverpool. Of Wordsworth, whom he saw on August 25th, he says with gentle sarcasm : " He was so benevolently anxious to impress upon me my social duties as an American citizen, that he accompanied me near a mile from his house, talking vehemently, and ever and anon stopping short to imprint his words." It appears, however, from the fuller report in " English Traits," that Wordsworth said many wise things about America, one among others which long seemed a paradox, that Americans needed a civil war to teach the necessity of knitting the social ties stronger. He solemnized Goethe's birthday by vituperating " Wilhelm Meister" : his criticism is one of the most curious examples extant of the inability of the merely ethical temper to enter into the artist's sympathetic observation of life. He had relieved his mind by throwing the book across the room, and, notwithstanding his

promise to Emerson, it may be doubted whether he
ever picked it up again. The moment was certainly unpro-
pitious for a return to the charge. Wordsworth's eyes were
grievously inflamed, and his physiognomy was disfigured
by green goggles. Carlyle he thought sometimes insane,
but this was probably merely a second-hand opinion.
He preferred Lucretius to Virgil ; and yet Virgil was
almost the only poet to whom he paid the compliment
of translation. That Wordsworth should recite his own
poetry was inevitable, and at first Emerson was "near to
laugh. But recollecting that I had come thus far to see
a poet, and that he was chanting poems to me, I saw
that he was right and I was wrong, and gladly gave myself up to hear." On the whole Wordsworth "made the
impression of a narrow and very English mind ; of one
who paid for his rare elevation by general tameness and
conformity. Off his own beat, his opinions were of no
value." But on his beat he was profound and inspiring,
as when he told his visitor that "whatever was didactic
might perish quickly, but whatever combined a truth with
an affection was κτημα ἐς ἀεί, good to-day and good for
ever."

At Liverpool, Emerson spent nine days weather bound,
but solaced by the company of Jacob Perkins, the in-
ventor of the steam gun, who prophesied that the ocean
would be navigated by merchant steamers, "but there is
a great deal to be done first." Within five years, however, the first steam-ship crossed the Atlantic. Emerson's
voyage in a sailing packet occupied one month and five
days. He had time to sum up the results of his visit to
Europe, and question himself what manner of man he

was taking back to America. His travel had been of the highest value to him, more than he quite knew. Not only had his views expanded and his mind imbibed new ideas, but he had profited by detachment from the concerns of a limited community and an isolated church. Though crude in form, his thoughts committed to paper on shipboard have a largeness and liberty not attained by him before. He also began to feel dimly that he might have a message to deliver to Europe as well as to America. The wise man, coming to teach, often remains to learn ; but sometimes the case is reversed, and so in a certain degree it was with Emerson. "The great men of England," he wrote, " are singularly ignorant of religion." This dictum would have astonished Wordsworth and Coleridge. Swedenborg met in the other world with certain individuals who seemed to themselves comely men, " but to the angels they appeared like dead horses."

Upon arriving in America, Emerson went to live with his mother at Newton, near Boston, and immediately found himself largely in request both as preacher and lecturer. Disencumbered of every special tie, the independence of his position corresponded to the enlargement of his views ; he could speak to his former flock like one emancipated.

" Man begins to hear a voice that fills the heavens and the earth, saying that God is within him ; that there is the celestial host. I find this amazing revelation of my immediate relation to God, a solution of all the doubts that oppressed me. I recognize the distinction of the outer and the inner self ; the double consciousness that within this erring, passionate, mortal self sits a supreme, calm, immortal mind, whose powers I do not know ; but it is stronger than I ; it is wiser than I; it never approved me in any wrong ; I seek counsel of it in my doubts ; I repair to it in my dangers ; I pray to it in my undertakings. It seems to me the face which the Creator uncovers to his child."

He concluded that this " increased clearness of the spiritual sight " must put an end to all that was " technical, allegorical, parabolical " in religious teaching, thus raising up fresh obstacles to his return to the regular groove of his profession. These were increased when the Quakers of New Bedford, with whose spirituality he felt the deepest sympathy, imbued him with a dislike, not merely to set forms of prayer, but to public prayer of any kind without prompting from on high. His views have been much misrepresented, but he himself said, " As well might a child live without its mother's milk as a soul without prayer." His position, however, was evidently inconsistent with a stated ministerial charge, and, after the offer of a pastorate at New Bedford had struck upon this rock, Emerson, though still not refusing to preach, and, in fact, preaching regularly for some years to a small congregation, seems to have esteemed himself a layman. He was now beginning to find his proper field in the lyceum and lecture-hall. His first lectures were scientific. Without any profound acquaintance with science, he knew enough to impart elementary information to an average audience. In dealing with higher matters he showed how immensely the man of science gains by being

also a man of thought. "The deeper a man's insight into
the spiritual laws, the more intense will be his love of the
works of nature. It is the wonderful charm of external
nature that man stands in a central connection with it
all." This fitted well with the doctrine of evolution,
which, without endeavouring to explain the process, he
assumed to be sufficiently established by the anatomical
evidence of gradual development. "Man is no upstart
in the creation. His limbs are only a more exquisite
organization—say rather the finish—of the rudimental
forms that have been already sweeping the sea and
creeping in the mud. The brother of his hand is even
now cleaving the Arctic Sea in the fin of the whale, and
innumerable ages since was pawing the marsh in the
flipper of the saurian." A view afterwards condensed
into his memorable couplet—

> " Striving to be man, the worm
> Mounts through all the spires of form."

But he was far from regarding the progress of development as the result of a chance collision of atoms, or a
blind struggle for existence. With clear good sense he
pointed out the indications of self-conscious forethought
in the universe—"the preparation made for man in the
slow and secular changes and melioration of the surface
of the planet; his house built, the grounds laid out, the
cellar stocked."

In October, 1834, Edward Emerson, "brother of the
brief but blazing star," died in Porto Rico, to the deep
grief of Waldo and the intense disappointment of many

who had regarded the younger brother as by far the more brilliant of the two.

> " His from youth the leader's look
> Gave the law which others took,
> And never poor beseeching glance
> Shamed that sculptured countenance."

Edward, however, had said, " The real lion of the tribe of Judah is at home." His gifts appear rather to have fitted him for an active than a literary life; only one short poem, and no written meditation, came of the long decline he bore with heroic constancy. Charles, a younger brother of scarcely inferior promise, was engaged to a lady at Concord, and this perhaps had its influence in leading Mrs. Emerson's uncle, the now almost nonagenarian Dr. Ripley, the pastor of the town, to offer Mrs. Emerson and Waldo a home in the Old Manse, celebrated by Hawthorne, and which seems to have had a genius for growing old, seeing that in Hawthorne's own day it was younger than its late occupant. Its picturesque outline is given in Mr. Sanborn's paper in *Scribner's Monthly.* They went there in October, 1834. Ere long Emerson himself became engaged, and it was necessary to look out for a house of his own. He " dodged the doom of building, and bought the Coolidge house in Concord. It is a mean place." It does not appear mean in the view published by Mr. Sanborn, which justifies his description of it "as a modest, homelike, comfortable residence "—not unlike, it may be added, except for its wooden material, the half-marine, half-rustic villa that may be espied hiding itself in a plantation near

many a quiet English watering-place. The scenery of the
neighbourhood, though not striking, sufficed a poet of
Wordsworthian sympathies who had sat down in the shadow
of Etna without ecstasy, and mainly sought to glean from
Nature "the harvest of a quiet eye." "It might seem,"
he said, "to bright eyes a dull rabbit-warren," but it gave
him what he wanted. Hawthorne, coming afterwards to
dwell in the old manse of Dr. Ripley where Emerson had
dwelt before him, has depicted the landscape from
several different points of view, and notwithstanding his
wrath at the muddiness of the slow river, "too lazy to
keep itself clean," the general impression is eminently
pleasing. He paints the semicircular sweep of the stream,
looking under certain aspects, for all its impurity, like a
strip of sky let into the earth; the broad, peaceful
meadows, of which it was the central line, the bordering
ridges swelling forward or sloping gradually back, with a
white village here and there embowered in its wood-
lands—Dutch nature spiritualized by Western influences.
Not far away was Walden Pond, the sylvan lake more
indissolubly associated with Thoreau's name than even
with Emerson's, often as he

> " Smote the lake to please his eye
> With the beryl beam of the broken wave,
> And flung in pebbles, well to hear
> The moment's music which they gave."

It was natural, too, that he should feel as a patriot
towards Concord, remembering his descent from its
founder, and that his fellow-townsmen (who also conferred upon him the dignity of hog-reeve) should call

upon him for an address on their second centennial anniversary, September, 1835. With simple but striking eloquence he discoursed of the heroic passages of the history of Concord, especially the hardships and renunciations of the original settlers. "Many were their wants, but more their privileges. The light struggled in through windows of oiled paper, but they read the Word of God by it. They were fain to make use of their knees for a table, but their limbs were their own. Their religion was sweetness and peace amidst toil and tears." Coming down to later times, he could tell his audience how "the first organized resistance to the British arms was made about half a mile from this spot;" how he himself had found within the last few days a narrative of the fight in the handwriting of his grandfather, then pastor, and himself a martyr to the cause of independence, and an entry in an almanack in that ancestor's handwriting: "This month remarkable for the greatest events of the present age." Speaking of his researches among the town records, "which must ever be the fountains of all just information respecting your character and customs," he could say: "They exhibit a pleasing picture of a community almost exclusively agricultural, where no man has much time for words in his search after things, of a community of great simplicity of manners, and of a manifest love of justice. These soiled and musty books are luminous and electric within. The old town-clerks did not spell very correctly, but they contrive to make pretty intelligible the will of a free and just community."

On the next anniversary of the Battle of Lexington, April 19, 1836, the monument erected to commemorate the birth of American independence was inaugurated by verses from the pen of Emerson, destined, like the shot he celebrates, to be "heard round the world "—

> " By the rude bridge that arched the flood,
>   Their flag to April's breeze unfurled,
> Here once the embattled farmers stood,
>   And fired the shot heard round the world.
>
> The foe long since in silence slept ;
>   Alike the conqueror silent sleeps ;
> And Time the ruined bridge has swept
>   Down the dark stream which seaward creeps.
>
> On this green bank, by this soft stream,
>   We set to-day a votive stone ;
> That memory may their deed redeem,
>   When, like our sires, our sons are gone.
>
> Spirit, that made those heroes dare
>   To die, and leave their children free,
> Bid Time and Nature gently spare
>   The shaft we raise to them and thee."

Two days after Emerson's Concord oration, he " drove over to Plymouth, and was married." His wife—Lydia, or as he chose to call her Lidian, Jackson, sister to Dr. Charles Jackson, of anæsthetic fame—has made his renown her obscurity. Her modest figure occasionally flits across the background of his public career, and the few letters from him to her which have found their way into print reveal both affection and the assurance of sympathy. "The soul of faith," was the character he gave her. He had expected to enlarge the house for the joint occupancy

of Charles Emerson and his bride, but the new chambers
were never needed. In April, 1836, Emerson went south-
ward with Charles, who needed a milder climate. He left
him in New York apparently better, was sharply summoned
back, and arrived too late. "I shall have my sorrow to
myself," he exclaims, "for if I speak of him I shall be
thought a fond exaggerator. How much I saw through
his eyes! I feel as if my own were very dim." There
is but one opinion as to Charles Emerson's promise,
though he was less conspicuously brilliant than Edward.
Like Edward, he was rather an orator and a man of
action than a writer; "he looked forward," says Emerson,
"to the debates of the senate on great political questions,
as to his first and native element. And with reason, for
in extempore debate his speech was music, and the pre-
cision, the flow, and the elegance of his discourse equally
excellent. His memory was a garland of immortal
flowers, and all his reading came up to him as he talked."
"After the death of his brothers," says Mr. Cooke,
"Emerson took a much greater interest in public matters,
feeling that his duties were increased, and that he must
fill more perfectly his place as a citizen."

Emerson's main intellectual occupation during these
two years of domestic-enrichment and bereavement was
the slow composition of his epoch-making tract on
Nature; but he also found time for public discourse.
He gave five biographical lectures at Boston on Michael
Angelo, Luther, Milton, George Fox, and Burke. Those
on Michael Angelo and Milton are extant in *The North
American Review*. Emerson himself thought them un-
worthy of preservation, and he was right. They were

well adapted for their immediate purpose, but have no special originality or force. Ten lectures on English literature delivered in the Masonic Temple, Boston, have not been printed, but are fully analyzed by Mr. Cabot. Emerson's connection with the pulpit was resumed for a time : for three years he preached regularly to a small flock at East Lexington—a work of necessity on the showing of one of the sheep, who declared that the simple people laboured under a positive incapacity of under-standing any one but Mr. Emerson. And, in fact, the charge of obscurity so frequently brought against Emerson is exceedingly unjust as respects individual sentences. His thought is transparent and almost chillingly clear, "he casts forth his ice like morsels." The obscurity, when there is any, arises from the want of logical sequence in his argument, and of tone and keeping amid the mass of glittering beauties, not duly subordinate to the general impression.

Emerson was now called upon to deal editorially with a Prophet. Admiration for Carlyle had made him subscribe to *Fraser* as long as "Sartor Resartus" appeared in it, and his critical faculty was thus subjected to the severest test to which such faculty can be exposed in the summons to recognize an entirely new order of excellence. To this he failed to respond. It is a remarkable phenomenon, continually verified, that minds of unusual subtlety and penetration seem to labour under an incapacity for appreciating the sublime. The instrument of such minds often seems rather the spectroscope which dissects a single beam in a darkened room than the telescope which ranges infinite space from the summit of the mountain. The intellect which finds thoughts too deep for tears in the flower responds with no thrill of agitation to the tempest; the perception which detects the microscopic though real beauties of a Clough cannot see the splendour which invests heaven and earth in the verse of a Shelley. Emerson's was such a mind: the sublimity of "Sartor" was lost upon him; and that other defect in his mental constitution, which, while allowing him a vein of epigrammatic humour, left him insensible to the glorious mirth of an Aristophanes or a Dickens, abolished for him the second element of greatness in "Sartor," its humour. Its philosophical truth remained, and this Emerson appreciated, but the form and style were sore trials to him. "O Carlyle!" he exclaims in his diary, "the merit of glass is not to be seen, but to be seen through; but every crystal and lamina of the Carlyle glass shows." A sound criticism, if the purpose of "Sartor" had been to make things plain to the meanest capacity. Men of poetical gifts like Emerson and Carlyle are on safer ground when they admire than when they blame: as with Swedenborg's angels, it is only when they affirm a truth that their wands blossom in their hands. As the importer of the only copy in America, he nevertheless stood towards the book *in loco parentis*; and when Dr. Le Baron Russell defrayed the cost of the first transatlantic edition, Emerson contributed the preface. His introduction was deemed by the enthusiastic timid and superfluously apologetic; but he felt that he was breaking his own rule "to do nothing which I cannot do with my whole heart." Soon *The North American Review* came to the rescue, and Emerson could report to Carlyle, "I have quite lost my plume as your harbinger."

After editing "Sartor" Emerson turned seriously to the publication of his own gospel. His tract on "Nature," the most intense and quintessential of his writings, and the first in which he came forward teaching as one having authority, seems to have been commenced even before he took up his residence at Concord, but was not completed till August, 1836. It was published in the following month, without at first attracting much attention. It proved, however, a seed implanted in a fissure of the crumbling New England theology, whose unnoticed expansion had force enough to shatter the whole fabric. By its conception—not of course original with Emerson or peculiar to him—of external Nature as an incarnation of the Divine Mind, it utterly abolished most of the controversies which had agitated the intellect of America, and in particular caught up the philosophy of Jonathan Edwards, that masterpiece of earthly reasoning, into a heaven of which Edwards had never dreamed. The rigid despotism of an extra-mundane ruler now appeared the free agency of an indwelling power: and similarly, without infringing a single moral rule, the stiff morality of the Unitarians was transfigured and glorified until it hardly knew itself. At the same time God and Nature were by no means confounded; the former was recognized as the infinite cause, the latter as the infinite effect: and though a cause without an effect is certainly inconceivable, the formal duality is made not less clear than the substantial unity. Man was represented as the intermediate phase of being, tending upwards or downwards, according as he inclines to Divine freedom or natural necessity. To quote Mr. Cabot's analysis, " regarded as part of nature, he is the victim of his environment: of race, temperament, sex, climate, organization. But man is not simply a part of nature, not mere effect, but, potentially, shares the cause. When he submits his will to the Divine inspiration, he becomes a creator in the finite. If he is disobedient, if he would be something in himself, he finds all things hostile and incomprehensible. As a man is, so he sees and so he does. When we persist in disobedience, the inward ruin is reflected in the world about us. When we yield to the remedial force of spirit, then evil is no more seen." Evil, then, may be regarded as the price man pays for being above Nature; and as Emerson could not deem this as by any means too high, he was necessarily an optimist to the extent, at least, of maintaining that, much as we suffer from moral evil, we should be worse off without it. Without it we should be but a part of the machinery of Nature; its existence is a proof of our liberty, which involves the liberty to rise superior to it. "As when the summer comes from the south, the snowbanks melt, and the face of the earth becomes green before it, so shall the advancing spirit create its ornaments along its path, and carry with it the beauty it visits, and the song which enchants it; it shall draw beautiful faces, and warm hearts, and wise discourses, and heroic acts around its way, until evil is no more seen." This prophecy was confirmed by cogent though highly poetical reasoning, an appeal to admitted facts showing that Nature and Man actually were in sympathy. "When a noble act is done—perchance in a scene of great natural beauty; when Leonidas and his three hundred martyrs consume one day in dying, and the

sun and the moon come each and look at them once in
the steep defile of Thermopylæ; when Arnold Winkelried,
in the high Alps, under the shadow of the avalanche,
gathers in his side a sheaf of Austrian spears to break the
line for his comrades : are not these heroes entitled to
add the beauty of the scene to the beauty of the deed ?
When the bark of Columbus nears the shore of America;
before it, the beach lined with savages fleeing out of all
their huts of cane ; the sea behind, and the purple
mountains of the Indian Archipelago around, can we
separate the man from the living picture? . . . In private
places, among sordid objects, an act of truth or heroism
seems at once to draw to itself the sky as its temple, the
sun as its candle. Nature stretcheth out her arms to
embrace man, only let his thoughts be of equal greatness. Willingly does she follow his steps with the rose
and the violet, and bend her lines of grandeur and grace
to the decoration of her darling child. Only let his
thoughts be of equal scope, and the frame will suit the
picture. A virtuous man is in unison with her works,
and makes the central figure of the visible sphere."
Man, then, had but to place himself in a right relation
with God and Nature, and the inextricable puzzles of
liberty and necessity would be solved of themselves. If
the logical connection of the treatise was not always very
close, it is to be remembered that it was the work of a
poet, and that the ideas it embodied were for the most
part so exquisite and ennobling as to be their own best
credentials. The most fascinating part of the little book
was the alluring delineation of natural beauty ; the
most substantially valuable, the resolute assertion of the

identity of natural and spiritual law; the convertibility of natural and spiritual forces; every existence in nature the counterpart of an existence in the world of mind; every natural truth a truth also in human life. In the pregnant phrase of George Herbert, quoted by the writer—

> "Man is one world, and hath
> Another to attend him."

CHAPTER IV

A CERTAIN boisterous zone of ocean is known to the seaman as "the roaring forties." The future historian of this century may dwell on "the still thirties," as a decade more pregnant with intellectual than with political revolution. In 1830 occurred the great debate on fixity of type between Cuvier and Geoffroy Saint Hilaire, which Goethe thought infinitely more important than the Revolution of July. In 1831 Darwin departed on his eventful voyage, "Sartor Resartus" was written, and the British Association founded. In 1835 appeared the epoch-making works of Strauss and Tocqueville; statistics first assumed the dignity of a science; and the names of Copernicus and Galileo vanished from the Index Expurgatorius. In March of the same year Emerson speaks to Carlyle of a projected journal to be called the Transcendentalist. The christening nevertheless, Hibernically, perhaps mystically, preceded the birth, for it was not until September, 1836—the month which the publication of "Nature" would alone have sealed as an epoch—that Emerson, Dr. Hedge, George Ripley, and an unnamed companion, meeting on occasion of the second centennial anniversary of Harvard College, "chanced to confer on the state of current opinion in theology and philosophy, which we agreed in thinking very unsatisfactory." The upshot was a larger meeting of some dozen "like-minded seekers," at George Ripley's house in Boston, followed by a somewhat larger gathering at Emerson's own, to which others succeeded, and by and by the participants got the name of Transcendentalists. How they came by it, Dr. Hedge, our witness, does not know; not, he apprehends, on the ground of any special acquaintance with Kant's transcendental philosophy, seeing that no one knew anything about it except himself, and he will not affirm that he knew enough for a dozen. But Kant's name must have been heard in New England, for in 1833 Emerson told Wordsworth that all Boston was talking about Victor Cousin, which brilliant Frenchman had undoubtedly profited by his opportunities of studying the philosophy of Germany when he happened to be imprisoned in that country. Mr. Freeman Clarke gives another name, and another reason. "We called ourselves the club of the like-minded. I suppose because no two of us thought alike." "Or rather, we may say," adds Mr. Cabot with justice, "because, in spite of all differences of opinion, they were united by a common impatience of routine thinking." In any case, the designation of transcendentalist was not one to be ashamed of. "The transcendental philosophy," says Frothingham, "is the philosophy that is built on these necessary and universal principles, the primary laws of mind, which are the ground of absolute truth." Since these meetings began and ceased the special dogma of Transcendentalism proper, the assertion of knowledge, independent of experience, has been, one may say, both proved and disproved. Observation, more fruitful of

result than speculation, has, by the study of the phenomena
of heredity, triumphantly vindicated the doctrine of innate
ideas as respects the individual, while overthrowing it
as respects the race. It is certain that the human mind
at birth is by no means a sheet of blank paper; it is
equally certain that the impressions which it brings into
the world are the result of the accumulated experiences
of its progenitors. But though the discovery might have
silenced the controversialists on both sides in Emerson's
time, it would not have quelled the controversy. The
dispute was only one item among large issues. Was
utility the measure of right? Could truth be apprehended by intuition? Could religion be identified with
the letter of a book, or proved by a miracle? The affir-
mative and negative of any of these propositions seemed
à priori, equally rational; if Emerson and his followers
speedily got a bad name with sober people, it was not that
their side of the question was intrinsically unreasonable,
but because it was naturally congenial to the more
imaginative, and therefore the more impulsive and refrac-
tory. "Your accomplished friend," said a denizen of
Brook Farm, "would hoe corn all Sunday if I would
let him, but all Massachusetts could not make him do it
on Monday." Hence no school of thought was less sympathetic with Emersonianism than that in whose bosom it
had been developed into a creed—the Unitarian. "The
Unitarians of New England," says Frothingham, "good
scholars, careful reasoners, clear and exact thinkers,
accomplished men of letters, humane in sentiment, sincere in moral intention, belonged, of course with individual exceptions [such as Channing], to the class which

looked without for knowledge, rather than within for inspiration." It was to this habit of mind, and not to any theological differences, that Channing referred when he said, "I am little of a Unitarian." Unitarianism, in fact, had worked itself out, as Romanism and Calvinism had done before it. It had brought Christianity to such perfection that, as an admirer of Paley said, "it could be written out at examinations." And now the restless spirit of man, discontented with even this great result, was protesting that here it could find no abiding tabernacle.

In the winter of 1836 Emerson followed up his discourse on Nature by a course of twelve lectures on "The Philosophy of History," a considerable portion of which eventually became embodied in his Essays. From the abstract preserved by Mr. Cabot, the connection with history would seem to have been but remote ; nor is the connection of the lectures among themselves very apparent. The most important was that on Religion, which dwelt forcibly on "the great fact of the unity of the mind in all individual men." This, said Emerson, we learn from the sense of duty. "I seek my satisfaction at my neighbour's cost, and I find that he has an advocate in my own breast, interfering with my private action, and persuading me to act, not for his advantage or for that of all others, for it has no reference to persons, but in obedience to the dictate of the general mind. Virtue is this obedience, and religion is the accompanying emotion, the thrill at the presence of the universal soul." He went on to say that the attempt to embody this emotion in an outward form made the Church, but as "the truest state of thought rested in becomes false," the

Church was continually lapsing into unbelief, and as continually being recovered from it by " the light rekindling in some obscure heart." " Only a new Church is alive." A man who thus taught need not have wondered that his " one doctrine, the infinity of the private man," was only accepted " as long as I call the lecture Art, or Politics, or Literature, or the Household. The moment I call it Religion people are shocked, though it be only the application of the same truth which they receive everywhere else." Every Church is sufficiently alive to resent being told that it is dead ; and the less the vitality the greater the resentment. In June, 1837, he tried the experiment of preaching in the pulpit of his his friend, Dr. Farley, " a sermon precisely like one of his lectures in style." " After returning home," says Dr. Farley, " I found Emerson with his head bowed in his hands, which were resting on his knees. He looked up and said, ' Now tell me honestly, plainly, just what you think of that service.' I replied that before he was half through I had made up my mind that it was the last time he should have that pulpit. ' You are right,' he rejoined, ' and I thank you. On my part before I was half through I felt out of place.' " He did not mean, as Mr. Cabot remarks, that he was out of place in the pulpit when he could find a sympathising congregation, for ten years had yet to pass ere he should preach his last sermon. But the pulpit was no longer to be his platform, the Lyceum had definitely gained what the Church had lost ; and it must be added that in this particular aspect the whole spiritual tendency of the age was for the moment incarnated in Emerson. Different indeed was the reception which

Literature, as impersonated in the Phi Beta Kappa Society, gave him on his next public appearance, the delivery of his oration on " Man Thinking, or the American Scholar," August 31, 1837. " It was," says Mr. Lowell, " an event without any former parallel in our literary annals, a scene to be always treasured in the memory for its picturesqueness and its inspiration. What crowded and breathless aisles, what windows clustering with eager heads, what enthusiasm of approval, what grim silence of foregone dissent ! " This great effect was no doubt partly due to the Fourth of July quality pervading the oration, which Dr. Holmes calls " our intellectual Declaration of Independence." " We were," says Mr. Lowell, " still socially and intellectually moored to English thought till Emerson cut the cable and gave us a chance at the dangers and glories of blue water." Americans felt inspirited and flattered by the assurance the discourse breathed that their literature need no longer be imitative ; that they need but rise to the level of their opportunities and duties as a free people, and their literature would rise along with them. The excellent counsel to the individual student, bursting forth in epigrammatic flashes which seemed paradoxes until reflection proved them aphorisms, also told for much. (" Books are for the scholar's idle times." "Action is with the scholar subordinate, but it is essential." "The scholar is one who raises himself from private considerations." " He, and he only, knows the world.") But these things were only subsidiary to the main purpose of the discourse, the proclamation of the oneness of mankind, and the omnipresence of God. " The near explains the far. The drop is a small ocean.

A man is related to all nature. This perception of the worth of the vulgar is fruitful in discoveries. Let me see every trifle bristling with the polarity that ranges it instantly as an eternal law; and the shop, the plough, and the ledger referred to the like cause by which light undulates and poets sing; and the world lies no longer a dull miscellany and lumber-room, but has form and order; there is no trifle, there is no puzzle; but one design unites and animates the farthest pinnacle and the lowest trench. . . . The dread of man and the love of man shall be a wall of defence and a wreath of joy around all. A nation of men will for the first time exist, because each believes himself inspired by the Divine Soul which also inspires all men."

In addressing his fellow-students, Emerson spoke *urbi;* but when his speech was directed *orbi*, he proved that this faith in the inspiration of all men by the Divine Soul was no idle figure of speech with him. He deemed that Idealism might be preached with good hope of acceptance even to bankers. In a passage from a subsequent lecture entitled "Transcendentalism," recalling and rivalling the finest pages of "Sartor Resartus," he says:

"How easy it is to show the materialist that he also is a phantom walking and working amid phantoms, and that he need only ask a question or two beyond his daily questions to find his solid universe proving dim and impalpable before his sense! The sturdy capitalist, no matter how deep and square on blocks of Quincy granite he lays his foundations of his banking house

or Exchange, must set it at last not on a cube corre-
sponding to the angles of his storehouse, but on a mass
of unknown materials and solidity, red-hot or white-hot,
perhaps, at the core; which rounds off to an almost
perfect sphericity, and lies floating in soft air, and goes
spinning away, dragging bank and banker with it at the rate
of thousands of miles an hour, he knows not whither,
—a bit of bullet now glimmering now darkling through a
small cubic space on the edge of an unimaginable pit of
emptiness. And this wild balloon, in which his whole
venture is embarked, is just an emblem of his whole
state and faculty. Ask him why he believes that an
uniform experience will continue uniform, or on what
grounds he founds his faith in his figures, and he will
perceive that his mental fabric is built up on just as
strange and quaking foundations as his proud edifice
of stone."

The course on Human Culture delivered in the following winter appears from Mr. Cabot's analysis to have been
an expansion of a passage in " Man Thinking." " The
main enterprise of the world for splendour, for extent, is
the upbuilding of a man." Thus, inverting the obvious
truth that the individual exists by and for the universe,
he showed that there was also a sense in which it might
be said that the universe existed by and for the individual.
In his next important public appearance he ventured on
no such daring inversion, but by merely following out a
tendency of thought already widely diffused, involved
himself in what would have proved a sharp controversy for one controversially given. The graduating

Divinity class of Cambridge invited him to deliver the customary discourse upon their entering on the ministry. On July 15, 1838, he appeared before them, his breast a mine of perilous stuff. His lonely meditations had been much exercised with the questions of the infallibility of Christ and the reality of miracles, and on both points he had been more orthodox than he then was. To the former he had alluded significantly in a passage in "Man Thinking." "The man has never lived that can feed us ever. The human mind cannot be enshrined in a person who shall set a barrier on any one side to this unbounded, unboundable empire. It is one central fire, which, flaming now out of the lips of Etna, lightens the capes of Sicily; and now, out of the throat of Vesuvius, illuminates the towers and vineyards of Naples. It is one light which beams out of a thousand stars. It is one soul which illuminates all men." Of the miracles attributed to Christ he had, in 1834, expressed himself doubtfully. "I suppose he wrought them. It has not yet been shown that the account is only the addition of credulous and mistaking love." This was to be expected: no mind was ever less competent than Emerson's to appreciate the weight of historical evidence for or against any alleged fact, or more indifferent to the test, or more impatient of the office. But in his own sphere of the spiritual, his opinion was sufficiently decided. "I should be well content to lose them. Indeed I should be glad. No person capable of perceiving the force of spiritual truth but must see that the doctrines of the teacher lose no more by this than the law of gravity would lose if certain facts alleged to have taken place did not take place." The excrescence of 1834 had become an ulcer by 1838. "The word Miracle," he told his hearers, "as pronounced by Christian Churches, gives a false impression, it is Monster. It is not one with the blowing clover and the falling rain." On the other point he was equally explicit: "Do not degrade the life and dialogues of Christ by insulation and peculiarity. Let them lie as they befell, alive and warm, part of the landscape, and of the cheerful day. . . . Friends enough you shall find who will hold up to your emulation Wesleys and Oberlins, Saints and Prophets. Thank God for these good men, but say, 'I also am a man.'" The mistake of continuing to yield a professional assent to what was not really believed had, the speaker thought, infected religion with unreality; and the staple of his discourse was a powerful description of its decay and an urgent appeal to his hearers to redeem it by being real, not merely professional men; not preachers from whose preaching it could not be inferred whether they were freeholders or paupers, fathers or childless, but such as "converted life into truth." The remedy for the deformities of the Church was first, soul; and second, soul; and evermore, soul. It did not, perhaps, occur to him that such a clerisy as he desiderated would soon have claimed to govern the country, and would have left no room for the journalists and politicians to whom that task had been assigned by Providence. The discourse is, in truth, the cry of a soul thirsting for the water-springs, the protest of ideal aspiration against the inevitable limitations of humanity: it was struck off at a heat, and is well-nigh the only example of sustained passion in his writings. He had been less emphatic in what he called "a shriek of indignation," a remonstrance addressed a short time before to President Van Buren on the wrongs of the Indians. He might have turned the edge of the attacks upon his oration but for what Miss Peabody justly calls an extreme of gentlemanliness. A passage had been omitted for want of time, containing a not unneeded warning against making the new truth a fanaticism, "looking down on the head of all human culture; setting up against Jesus Christ every little self magnified." Miss Peabody begged him to restore it in the discourse as published. "No," said Emerson, "these gentlemen have committed themselves against what I did read, and it would not be courteous or fair to spring this passage upon them now."

The Divinity School address might have passed with slight notice if it had been delivered anywhere else; but the shepherds of Harvard could hardly be expected to allow the wolf to carry off the lambs in their very presence, even at the invitation of the innocents themselves. Andrews Norton, a great scholar and divine, but one for whom truth could not be tangible enough, pro-nounced an emphatic anathema upon it in *The Boston Daily Advertiser.* It was absurd, he said, to suppose that religious truth could be demonstrated or guaranteed without violations of natural law, or that Christianity could endure without belief in the miraculous. It is not for us to determine whether the Professor proved his

point, but if he did, the entire drift of thought since
his time warrants the remark that he did Christianity
a singular disservice :

> " Da miei amici mi guarda Dio :
> Da miei nemici mi guarderó io."

As concerned Emerson himself the article was an excom-
munication as crushing, though not as dramatically
impressive, as Spinoza's. He was handled in a different
spirit by the saintly Henry Ware, his former colleague in
the Second Church, who feared that his doctrine of the
universal soul tended to merge Deity in humanity. To his
gentle remonstrance Emerson characteristically replied :

> " I could not give an account of myself, if challenged.
> I could not possibly give you one of the arguments
> you covertly hint at, on which any doctrine of mine
> stands ; for I do not know what arguments are in
> reference to any expression of a thought. I delight in
> telling what I think, but if you ask me how I dare say so,
> or why it is so, I am the most helpless of mortal men. I
> do not even see that either of these questions admits
> of an answer. So that in the present droll posture of
> my affairs, when I see myself suddenly raised to the
> importance of a heretic, I am very uneasy when I
> advert to the supposed duties of such a personage, who
> is to make good his thesis against all comers. I cer-
> tainly shall do no such thing. I shall read what you
> and other good men write, as I have always done,
> glad when you speak my thoughts, and skipping the
> page that has nothing for me."

These lines show that Emerson had formed a just idea of his strength and his weakness. He could see, but he could not prove; he could announce, but he could not argue. His intuitions were his sole guide; what they revealed appeared to him self-evident; the ordinary paths by which men arrive at conclusions were closed to him. To those in spiritual sympathy with himself he is not only fascinating, but authoritative; his words authenticate themselves by the response they awake in the breast. But the reader who will have reasons gets none, save reason to believe that the oracle is an imposition. " He is not a philosopher," said one who conversed with him at this time, " he is a seer. If you see truth as he does, you will recognize him for a gifted teacher; if not, there is little or nothing to be said." This inability to comply with the apostolic precept by rendering a reason for the faith that was in him had obvious drawbacks, balanced by two great advantages. It spared him irritating controversy, and kept him an almost impersonal influence, exempt from the soils and smirches of the purest party-chief. "If it be true," he wrote at this time in his diary, "that the scholar is merely an observer, a dispassionate reporter, no partisan, his position is one of perfect immunity. To him no disputes can attach, he is invulnerable. The vulgar think he would found a sect and be installed and made much of. He knows better, and much prefers his melons and his woods." He was nevertheless always ready to respond to private inquirers, and only regretted that with the best intentions he could not but be to a certain extent insincere, " knowing that there are other words." He laments having been beguiled by

" friendly youths " into " a rambling exculpatory talk upon Theism," whereas he ought to have said that he had no language ; as he did in effect to an Episcopalian clergyman, his cousin Mr. Haskins. " When I speak of God I prefer to say It." " I confess," says Mr. Haskins, " that I was at first startled by this answer ; but as far as he explained his views in the conversation which followed, I could discover no difference between them and the commonly accepted doctrine of God's omnipresence." When asked by Mr. Haskins, on another occasion, " to define his views," he answered with greater deliberate- ness and longer pauses between his words than usual, " I am more of a Quaker than anything else. I believe in the still, small voice, and that voice is Christ within us."

The expansion of Emerson's intellectual horizon, and the prominent position which, would he would he not, he was driven to assume as a leader of thought, inevitably widened the sphere of his intimacies, and made Concord the resort of thinkers more or less exceptional or eccen- tric, " wearing their rue with a difference." Among them the most remarkable was Margaret Fuller, one of those Sibyls or Alruna women who really and truly do appear, although for one genuine instance there are a hundred and fifty pretenders. Margaret, however, was a true counterpart to the Rahels and Bettinas of Germany ; unlike the first, intelligible, though oracular ; unlike the second, neither capricious nor insincere. When Emerson first knew her, her character was in the fulness both of its force and its angularity, qualities greatly tempered in her latter years. Not one of the contributors to her patchwork biography has succeeded in conveying a living resemblance of her; Emerson does not even attempt a portrait. Indeed he must have entertained something of the feeling towards her with which Goethe and Schiller regarded Madame de Staël, save that the New England meteor "came to stay." "It is to be said," he bravely admits, "that Margaret made a disagreeable first impression upon most persons;" and when we learn in addition that "the problems that chiefly attracted her were Mythology and Demonology," the thought will arise that she must have been formidable as well as disagreeable. Yet, though Emerson paints no portrait, he does contrive to make us understand how much more Margaret was really interested in her fellow creatures than in these mystic fancies, which served to exercise a powerful imagination, while the real business of her life was intellectual-comradeship and spiritual sympathy. With her imperious disposition this sympathy must needs be measured by the degree in which she could charm the recipient into her own circle, and as Emerson's serene star never

> "Shot madly from its sphere
> To list this sea-maid's music : "

their mutual bond was less close than her ambition would have desired. "He seemed to her," says Mrs. Howe, borrowing Margaret's own figure, "the palm-tree in the desert, graceful and admirable, bearing aloft a waving crest, but spreading no sheltering and embracing branches." Their acquaintance nevertheless became, if not a spiritual, an intimate literary alliance, which neither had any reason to regret.

Another ally of the period, with whom Emerson sympathized more heartily, was "the innocent charlatan," Amos Bronson Alcott, who repaid the confidence accorded him with the fondest reverence. It is well for Alcott that he never fell into the hands of Dickens, to whom he would have been irresistible, but encountered nobody worse than Carlyle, who has photographed him for all time as "the good Alcott, with his long lean face and figure, with his grey worn temples and mild radiant eyes; all bent on saving the world by a return to acorns and the golden age." Emerson found in the self-taught, self-sustained, "peacefully irrefragable" Alcott, an authentic inlet of pure light from the universal soul; which rebuked the involuntary scepticism of depressed moods by demonstrating that spirituality was no figment of the imagination. "I might have learned to treat the Platonic world as cloudland had I not known Alcott, who is a native of that country." He was therefore indulgent when it proved that spirituality could not write a book, or describe a fact as it really was. He intends no slur when he goes so far as to speak of Alcott's "victims"; certain that the deluder himself was the first and the chief. In the Blake-like Jones Very he found another piece of pure gold, needing something of terrestrial alloy for general circulation among men. Very's rapt spiritual countenance bears the image and superscription of Divine enthusiasm, and his translucent sonnets —amber without a fly—remain to attest that his claims to inspiration were no pretence. Their form is that of Shakespeare's, under whose spell Very had fallen as he sought to solve the problem, knotty to him, how a man can be a genius without being a saint. Emerson's notes and memoranda on Very are an interesting study of the contact. of an enthusiastic, but perfectly sane mind, with another too weak to bear the visitations of Divine light. Like all prophets, Very was intolerant ; but unlike most, he could accommodate himself to reason, as Mahomet did to the mountain. "He seemed to expect from me a full acknowledgment of his mission, and a participation in the same. Seeing this, I asked him if he did not see that my thoughts and my position were constitutional, that it would be as false and impossible for me to say his things or try to occupy his ground as for him to usurp mine? After some frank and full explanation he conceded this. In dismissing him I seem to have discharged an arrow into the heart of society." Society thought so too, and locked Very up as a lunatic. Though for a season mentally disturbed and dazzled, Very was no lunatic, only one who really believed what others said they believed. After a while the world and he so adjusted their relations as to allow of his becoming, with some detriment to his poetical faculty, a very excellent clergyman. Another saint of similar type, stainless but flighty as the fabled bird of Paradise which has forfeited its foothold in ridding itself of its feet— William Henry Channing—was also a member of Emerson's circle, and has left a picture of him in his home. "I do confess myself fascinated. He had been before to me an icy pinnacle only, away in the ether, but as I came nearer I found there was verdure of sweet affections and the beauteous blossoms of lowly thoughts and common herbs around the base. His family delighted me; his fondness for his little boy, his tenderness towards his wife, the unaffected politeness and courtesy and the merry cheerfulness of the man did more to win me than all his lofty contemplations."

Among these figures, radiant with sincere, if sometimes ill-directed aspiration, moved at intervals a dark silent figure of spiritual nature too, but much more of a gnome than of a sylph. Nathaniel Hawthorne half-consciously contributed an element of tragedy to the Concord society ("I suppose he died of his painful solitude," Emerson afterwards wrote), and, quite unconsciously, an element of comedy. Wifely devotion should be too sacred for a smile, yet it is hard to resist something broader than a smile in contrasting the fascination which Mrs. Hawthorne supposes her husband to have exerted upon Emerson with Emerson's own frank avowal that he talked continually to Hawthorne in the hope that, for very shame's sake, Hawthorne would one day say something himself, which he never did. Evidently he had been insufficiently impressed by Emerson's maxim—"It is the one base thing to receive and not to give." They lived on neighbourly terms, but there could be no true sympathy between authors who so greatly underrated each other's work. Emerson, whose literary judgments when not absolutely right are apt to be absurdly wrong, calls work which might embody the accumulated experience of several lives, too young. Hawthorne, on his part, had too much imagination not to be sensitive to "the pure intellectual gleam" with which Emerson lit up the woodland paths around Walden

Pond. "Like the garment of a shining one," he says; nor did the "austere beauty" of Emerson's poetry repel him. But several passages in his notebooks reveal impatience at Emerson's intellectual aloofness, and in one suppressed at first, but injudiciously restored by his son, he describes Emerson as "stretching his hand out of cloudland in the vain search for something real." The Civil War was to show which of the two men more firmly grasped reality, but that time of fiery trial was not yet, and meanwhile Hawthorne sat by Emerson's hearth and drew the guests in charcoal. "Young visionaries," he says, "to whom just so much of insight had been imparted as to make life all a labyrinth around them, came to seek the clue that should lead them out of their self-involved bewilderment. Grey-headed theorists—whose systems, at first air, had imprisoned them in an iron framework—travelled painfully to his door, not to ask deliverance, but to invite his free spirit into their own thraldom. People that had lighted on a new thought, or a thought that they fancied new, came to Emerson, as the finder of a glittering gem hastens to a lapidary to ascertain its value."

Where Hawthorne saw fit *dramatis personæ* for his "Twice Told Tales," Emerson discerned the heirs of all the ages, the children of the kingdom.

"No one can converse much with different classes of society in New England without remarking the progress of a revolution. Those who share in it have no external organization, no badge, no creed, no name. They do not vote, or print, or even meet together. They do not know each other's faces or names. They are united only in a common love of truth and love of its work. They are of all conditions and constitutions. Of these acolytes, if some are happily born and well bred, many are no doubt ill-dressed, ill-placed, ill-made, with as many scars of hereditary vice as other men. Without pomp, without trumpet, in lonely and obscure places, in solitude, in servitude, in compunctions and privations, trudging beside the team in the dusty road, or drudging as hirelings in other men's cornfields, schoolmasters who teach a few children rudiments for a pittance, ministers of small parishes of the obscure sects, lone women in dependent condition, matrons and young maidens, rich and poor, beautiful and hard-favoured, without concert or proclamation of any kind, they have silently given in their several adherence to a new hope, and in all companies do signify a greater trust in the nature and resources of man than the laws or the popular opinions will well allow."

This fine passage is from the confession of faith prefixed by Emerson to "The Dial," which, under the editorship of Margaret Fuller, appeared as the organ of New England Transcendentalism, in July, 1840. The reality of the phenomena thus eloquently described was universally admitted, but others saw in them "the Pentecost of Shinar." And, unquestionably, a Babylonish dialect was not unfrequently heard, and Mrs. Hominy was no mere creation of the novelist's brain. It was probably she who inquired at a lecture: "Mr. Alcott, does omnipotence abnegate attribute?" Yet, as ever, the loving and hoping spirit went nearer the mark than the

sceptical and negative. " The Dial " has become a bye-
word for crazy mysticism, as Wordsworth became to his
own generation for namby-pamby, and with hardly more
reason. There is, no doubt, a good deal of the Orphic,
a good deal of the oracular ; some verse that will not
scan, and some prose that will not construe ; not a little
really well-composed rhetoric that is too plainly diluted
Emersonianism. But there are also many contributions
of sterling value, showing perfect sanity and sound
insight; others valuable even now for the information they
contain, and in their day welcome harbingers of intellectual changes to come ; there are fictions, such as W.
E. Channing's "Youth of the Poet and Painter," artless in
structure, but charming as prose poems ; and verses by
the same writer and others, wanting in finish, but wood-
notes wild of genuine poetic passion. " The Dial "
translated Schelling's introductory lecture to his last
philosophical course; published Keats's notes on Milton;
saved his brother George from undeserved oblivion ; and
showed by some happily rescued fragments what an
Emerson was lost in Charles. On the whole it will
compare most favourably with any similar rally of undis-
ciplined and unsalaried enthusiasm round a flag which
must of necessity attract eccentricity; and the wonder
is rather that so much ability should have been mustered
in support of such a venture from so limited a section
of New England culture. The real charm, however, is
not so much any special literary excellence, as the fresh,
disinterested, unworldly spirit, warrant of youth in the
present and large possibilities in the future.

Margaret Fuller bore the burden of " The Dial " as

long as she could, and in 1842 Emerson assumed it, though foreseeing that he should "rue the day of accepting such an intruder on my peace, such a consumer of my time. But you have played martyr a little too long alone; let there be rotation in martyrdom." He by no means belonged to the "able editor" species so enviously admired by Carlyle. On one occasion he stood out against a proffered contribution by Theodore Parker, which, being admitted at last, carried the number into a second edition. "The Dial's" pages, notwithstanding, owe much of the freshness which clings to them after half a century, to his love for bright and promising young persons, and their eagerness to be associated with him. His own contributions include the introduction already quoted, his "Man the Reformer" "Transcendentalist," "Young American," reviews of Landor and of Carlyle's "Past and Present"; among his poems, "Saadi," "The Snowstorm," "Wood Notes," "The Sphinx," and others. He was not only "The Dial's" editor, but its banker, and his connection with it cost him not only the worry he had foreseen, but several hundred dollars, not easily replaced by a philosopher or spared by the father of a family. In April, 1844, the doom of all journals that do not pay their contributors finally overtook "The Dial," and it expired with the precept in its mouth, "Energise about the Hecatic sphere." Years afterwards a quantity of unsold copies were discovered and sent to Emerson, who gave of them to all who would, and burned or wasted the remainder. Had they been preserved to this day they would have been a small fortune. Mr. Ireland is the envied possessor of a copy containing a list of the contributors in Emerson's hand-writing. The information thus imparted is made public property in Mr. Cooke's interesting article in "The Journal of Speculative Philosophy" for July, 1885, where biographical particulars respecting the principal contributors are also to be found.

"We are a little wild here," wrote Emerson to Carlyle, on October 30, 1840, "with numberless projects of social reform. Not a reading man but has his draft of a new community in his waistcoat pocket. I am gently mad myself." Socialism was indeed in the air of the time, and not wholly without reason. Even the staid George Combe, visiting America in 1839, was induced by the difficulties which he perceived to attach to the management of American households, to conjecture that the richer Americans might in time agree to solve them by co-operation. The practical outcome of this unrest was the establishment of Alcott's little and luckless com-munity at Fruitlands, and the more famed experiment at Brook Farm, immortalized in Hawthorne's "Blithedale Romance." It was inevitable that Emerson should be pressed to cast in his lot with the projectors, and, conscious of a certain responsibility towards professed followers, he felt compunction at hanging back. But he was an individual of individuals; a crystal isolated, infrangible, infusible; the last of mankind to be merged in a joint-stock association. He wisely determined that his service must consist for the present in standing still and waiting, and that he must needs "submit to the degra-dation of owning bank stock and seeing poor men suffer." By way of atonement he himself tried some experiments on a small scale. Feeling that he would be happier if his house sheltered more fellow-creatures, he offered the Alcotts free hospitality for a year, a scheme which fortunately came to nothing. He had always been remarkable for considerateness to his servants, and now tried to revive the patriarchal, feudal, and in a simple state of society most seemly institution of a common family board. But Louisa the maid would not sit down without Lydia the cook, and Lydia held that a cook, unlike her dishes, was never fit to come to table. He theorized upon the advantage of combining manual labour with literary composition, but experience soon convinced him that his fine speeches must be unsaid. All these things he regarded as, at most, counsels of perfection for the individual: he perceived that the impossible expectations of the rank and file must force the leaders into charlatanism, and touched the extravagances of Fourierism with playful satire. But he saw more deeply into it than those for whom it was quite enough that Fourier proposed to turn the seas into lemonade. " I regard these philanthropists as themselves the effects of the age in which we live, and, in common with so many other good facts, the efflorescence of the period, and predicting a good fruit that ripens. They were not the creators they believed themselves, but they were unconscious prophets of a true state of society : they were describers of that which is really being done. The large cities are phalansteries, and the theorists drew all their arguments from facts already taking place in our experience."

The Brook Farm adventure has been much misapprehended. Though inspired by Fourier's ideas, it was hardly a socialistic experiment. The freedom of the individual member was jealously guarded by its constitution. Members were not required to impoverish themselves, or resign the fruits of their earnings. It was especially Fourieristic in the stress laid upon culture and refinement, and one of the leading features was an excellent school. It hence attracted many considerably in need of such humanizing influences, and such profited largely by the opportunity; but, as Emerson shrewdly remarks, they came rather to learn than to work, "and were charged by the heads of the departments with a certain indolence and selfishness." It may be added that others came less to work than to play, and, what was worse, could not discover that their work, when they performed any, was attended by those ennobling effects on the character which theoretically ought to have accrued. "They scratched their heads sometimes, to see, was the hair turned wool?" On the other hand, the art of letter-writing was immensely cultivated, and plain people saw with astonishment that he who ploughed all day earned no more than he who looked out of the window. The scheme had a beautiful side, but it wanted reality. "What I am doing," says Emerson, most wisely, "may not be the highest thing to do in all the world, but while I am doing it I must think that it is, or I shall not do it with impunity." Brook Farm was little more than a highly intellectual picnic, and though it might have prolonged its existence indefinitely if it had not involved itself in industrial competition, its existence could have demonstrated nothing more than the agreeableness of association with agreeable company, and, which was certainly more important, the possibility of frank equality among different orders of society. To this, Emerson, a sharp observer and no indiscriminate panegyrist, may be accepted as a sufficient witness: "What knowledge of themselves and of each other, what various practical wisdom, what personal power, what studies of character, what accumulated culture, many of the members owed to it! What mutual measure they took of each other! It was a close union, like that in a ship's cabin, of clergymen, young collegians, merchants, mechanics, farmers' sons and daughters, with men and women of rare opportunities and delicate culture, yet assembled there by a sentiment which all shared—some of them hotly shared —of the honesty of a life of labour, and the beauty of a life of humanity. The yeoman saw refined manners in persons who were his friends, and the lady or the romantic scholar saw the continuous strength and faculty in people who would have disgusted them but that these powers were now spent in the direction of their own theory of life."

Even if Emerson had not been too much of an individualist to be deeply fascinated by co-operative schemes, he had long taken root in Concord. "When I bought my farm," he says, "I did not know what a bargain I had in the bluebirds, bobolinks, and thrushes, which were not charged in the bill. As little did I guess what sublime mornings and sunsets I was buying, what reaches of landscape, and what fields and lanes for a tramp. Still less did I know what good and true neighbours I was buying, men of strength and virtue, some of them now known the country through, but whom I had the

pleasure of knowing long before the country did." Other
neighbours of homelier note had an equal share of his
esteem; "not doctors of laws, but doctors of land,
skilled in turning a swamp or a sandbank into a fruitful
field." Hawthorne shows us the type of such an one:
"A short and stalwart and sturdy personage, of middle
age, with a face of shrewd and kind expression, and
manners of natural courtesy. He had a very free flow
of talk, and not much diffidence about his own opinions;
for, with a little induction from Mr. Emerson, he began
to discourse about the state of the nation, agriculture,
and business in general, uttering thoughts that had come
to him at the plough, and which had a sort of flavour
of the fresh earth about them." Such were the men by
whose homely wisdom Emerson loved to profit. "He is
a thinker," wrote Miss Martineau, who visited him in his
home, "without being solitary, abstracted, and unfitted
for the time. He is ready at every call of action. He
lectures to the factory people at Lowell when they ask.
He preaches when the opportunity is presented. He is
known at every house along the road he travels to and
from home by the words he has dropped, and the deeds
he has done." He attended the town-meetings with the
punctuality of a good citizen, though never participating
in the proceedings otherwise than by his vote. The tall,
slender, somewhat stooping figure, with narrow and
aquiline mould of countenance, brow not high but finely
modelled, deep-set eyes of such intense blue as has been
said to be only found in sea-captains, firm but sensitive
mouth, expression compounded of enthusiasm and kindly
shrewdness, as of a spirit entrusted with earthly interests,

mingled habitually with the twenty-five "solidest men" who made up the Concord Social Club. "Much the best society I have ever known," says Emerson; who adds that he never liked to be away from Concord on Tuesdays, when the club met. He probably found it a welcome relief to the strain of lonely thought, for the nature of his intellectual labour condemned him to solitude while it lasted; and meditation, if not actual composition, was his daily habit. He worked partly in his study, partly in the woods; and his account of his method to Mr. Haskins recalls the remark of Wordsworth's servant, that her master's library was outside, though his books were indoors. He went out early, he said, to hunt a thought, as a boy might hunt a butterfly, and, when successful, pinned the prize in his cabinet by entering it in his "Thought Book." Down the capture went, without any order, but when the need for essay or lecture arose, inquisition was made, and, by the aid of an index, the thoughts which fitted the subject were unearthed, polished, and linked together, like beads on a thread, Emerson said; but we, whose scrutiny the thread sometimes eludes, may agree with Mr. Haskins that comparison with a mosaic would have been more accurately descriptive. "I write," he tells Carlyle, "with very little system, and, as far as regards composition, with most fragmentary result—paragraphs incomprehensible, each sentence an infinitely repellent particle." Yet his "Method of Nature" was "written in the heat and happiness of a real inspiration:" and he speaks in "Circles" of "days when he was full of thoughts, and could write as he pleased." His peculiar genius rendered

him more independent of books than any other great
writer of his age. Depending so exclusively on his own
intuitions, his attitude towards other men was necessarily
somewhat that of the Caliph Omar towards the Alexandria
Library. He would deeply venerate them only when he
felt them to have gone beyond himself on some line
of his own, like Swedenborg or Montaigne. On the
whole, the chief use of books to him was the same as
the chief use he drew from his neighbours: to provide
himself with intellectual stimulus ("make my top spin,"
he called it), and keep his faculties from rusting. "They
inspire," he said, "or they are nothing." "He was never
comfortable away from them, and yet," says Mr. Cabot,
"they were pleasing companions, not counsellors, hardly
even intimates." No author seems at any time to have
exercised a controlling influence over him. He would
have been the same Platonist if Plato had never lived.
He pleased himself as well as Carlyle by reading through
the whole of Goethe at Carlyle's instance, but the traces
of his study would have been faint if Goethe had not
figured among his "Representative Men." Next to
poetry and mystic wisdom his favourite reading was
biography—"Plutarch," he says, "is the Doctor and
historian of heroism"—and he delighted in anecdote.
His literary taste, on the whole, was in one sense very
exclusive, rejecting Scott and Shelley as well as Aristophanes and Cervantes; in another very catholic, ranging
from the Bhagavat Ghita to Martial. In literature, as
in life, his aim was spiritual manhood, and he valued
books and men mainly as he found or deemed them
to conduce to it. What he said of "The Dial" was

true of himself: "Our resources are not so much
the pens of practised writers as the discourse of the
living, and the portfolios which friendship has opened
to us."

CHAPTER V.

IT is a testimony at once of Heaven's kindness to
Emerson, and of his own kindliness, that the only
misfortunes of his life which he felt as cruel wounds, were
the untimely deaths of those near and dear to him. He
had lost the first choice of his heart and his two marvellous brothers; and now, at the beginning of 1842, he
was to be more heavily afflicted still. If he was more
exemplary in any one relation of life than another it
was in the father's. The recollections of his surviving
children depict the ideal of wisdom, thoughtfulness, and
gentleness. It seemed as though the best of fathers had
been rewarded by the best of sons. Whether the remarkable promise of his first-born would have been fulfilled, it is of course impossible to say; but much might
reasonably be augured of a boy of five so affectionate as
to be his father's constant companion, and so considerate
as to spend hours in his study without one noisy out-
break. "A domesticated sunbeam," says a friend of the
house, "with his father's voice, but ·softened, and
beautiful dark blue eyes with long lashes." Emerson
himself names no family likeness; like the lover in his
own essay he "sees no resemblance except to summer

evenings and diamond mornings, to rainbows and the song of birds,"—

> " The wondrous child,
> Whose silver warble wild
> Outvalued every pulsing sound
> Within the air's cerulean round,—
> The hyacinthine boy, for whom
> Morn well might break and April bloom,—
> The gracious boy, who did adorn
> The world whereinto he was born,
> And by his countenance repay
> The favour of the loving Day."

Waldo Emerson was born October 30, 1836, and died January 27, 1842, after a few days' illness, from scarlet fever. Emerson's grief was the grief depicted on a Greek funeral monument, beautiful in its subdued intensity. He dissembled nothing from himself, not even his gratitude for every anodyne. "The innocent and beautiful," he wrote, "should not be sourly and gloomily lamented, but with music and fragrant thoughts and sportive recollections. . . . Life wears on, and ministers its undelaying and grand lessons, its uncontainable endless poetry, its stern dry prose of scepticism—like veins of cold air in the evening woods, quickly swallowed by the wide warmth of June—its steady correction of the rashness and short-sight of youthful judgments, and its pure repairs of all the rents and seeming ruin it operates in what it gave ; although we love the first gift so well that we cling long to the ruin, and think we will be cold to the new if new shall come. But the new steals on us like a star which rises behind our back as we walk, and we are borrowing gladly its light before we know the benefactor." In the thrilling threnody already quoted, after the stricken heart has long afflicted itself with the agonizing pictures traced by Memory and Fancy, Philosophy and Religion bring it consolation at last—

> "Fair the soul's recess and shrine,
>   Magic-built to last a season,
>   Masterpiece of love benign :
>   Fairer that expansive Reason
>   Whose omen 'tis, and sign.
>   Wilt thou not ope thy heart to know
>   What rainbows teach, and sunsets show?
>   Revere the Maker, fetch thine eye
>   Up to his style, and manners of the sky.
>   Not of adamant and gold
>   Built he heaven, stark and cold.
>   No, but a nest of bending reeds,
>   Flowering grass, and scented weeds ;
>   Or like a traveller's fleeing tent,
>   Or bow above the tempest bent ;
>   Built of tears and sacred flames,
>   And virtue reaching to its aims ;
>   Built of furtherance and pursuing,
>   Not of spent deeds, but of doing.
>   House and tenant go to ground,
>   Lost in God, in Godhead found."

"A few weeks ago," wrote Emerson to Carlyle, on occasion of his loss, "I accounted myself a very rich man, and now the poorest of all." "Your calm tone of deep, quiet sorrow," returned Carlyle, "coming in on the rear of your trivial worldly businesses, all punctually despatched and recorded too, as if the Higher and Highest had not been busy with you, tells me a sad tale." The "businesses" related principally to the publication of

Carlyle's works in America. It would be difficult to find a single action in Emerson's life not disinterested, and none were more beautifully inspired by unselfishness than his effort to assure Carlyle's works their due publicity and Carlyle his due reward. Carlyle's gratitude was warm, but it would have been warmer still if he had known the extent of his indebtedness. On August 3, 1839, Emerson wrote in his diary, "Carlyle's accounts have required what were for me very considerable advances, and so have impoverished me in the current months very much." On April 20th of the following year: "I suppose that I am now at the bottom of my wheel of debt, and shall not hastily venture lower. But how could I help printing 'Chartism,' sent to me for that express purpose, and with the encouragement of the booksellers? They will give T. C. fifteen cents per copy." On May 11, 1840, " J. Munroe and Co., in making out the account of T. C., find he was in my debt between six and seven hundred dollars, although some important amounts paid by me were not entered in the account." It must have been a relief to him when, after having published " Sartor," " The French Revolution," the " Miscellanies," " Chartism," and " Hero Worship," with no man to make him afraid, upon occasion of the arrival of " Past and Present " in 1843 he had to report to Carlyle that he had become worth pirating, inasmuch as " the cheap press has, within a few months, made a total change in our book-markets. Every English book of any name or credit is instantly converted into a newspaper or coarse pamphlet, and howled by a hundred boys in the streets." He nevertheless printed fifteen hundred copies at seventy-five cents, and for a few weeks succeeded in repelling the pirates, till a corsair calling himself Collyer, supposed to be another publisher's domino or dummy, bore down upon him with an edition at twelve cents and a half, and Emerson struck his flag, rejoiced that at least no money would be lost. Small remittances for Carlyle still crossed the Atlantic for some time longer, and he on his part could send Emerson twenty-four pounds on account of the English reprint of his Essays, notwithstanding the competition of "a scoundrel interloper, who prints on grey paper."

Even so, for the year preceding Emerson's great calamity had made him worth robbing. The first series of his Essays appeared in 1841. Up to this date he had been chiefly known as a lecturer, and although the imputation of heresy had helped his discourse before the Divinity class to a sale of a thousand copies, his reputation was still mainly local, and confined to the inner circles even of New England culture. But the Essays went wherever the English language was spoken, and the revelation of his name was also the revelation of his ripest power. They were not, like "Nature," too mystic and dithyrambic for the reader who valued himself on his common sense; nor, like the addresses on public occasions, were they in some measure of local and limited application. A considerable portion, indeed, had been originally delivered in the shape of lectures. "Love," "Friendship," "Prudence," "The Over-Soul," "Spiritual Laws," for instance, had been largely treated of in the courses for 1836 and 1837; and much material for a second series existed in these and in other courses.

But in this shape they had been blended with matter
of less value, and lacked the polish of perfect literary
expression which, as regarded the finish of individual
sentences, they now received to a degree rarely surpassed
by intellectual craftsmanship. The threefold test of lustre,
of durability, and of uniqueness, ranks them definitively
among the diamonds of literature. Diamonds, however,
are no material for statues ; and Emerson's writings, some
short poems excepted, prefer no claim to the yet higher
grace of logical unity and symmetrical completeness.
His usual method of literary work, already described,
precluded the composition of an essay in the proper
sense of the term. The thought that came to him to-
day generally bore slight affinity to the thought of yesterday or to-morrow. In exploring the notebooks where
these casual visitations of the Spirit lay stored like
autumnal leaves heaped in a forest dingle, Emerson
might find numerous analogies, but to fashion these into
a coherent whole were a task akin to that which Michael
Scott rightly judged too hard for the devil himself.
There is just enough unity of purpose and endeavour after
artistic construction in each several Essay to raise it
from the category of Table-Talks, the desultory record
of the wisdom of an Epictetus, a Luther, a Coleridge,
and to inscribe the collection upon the roll of great
unsystematic books, along with Marcus Aurelius and
Thomas à Kempis, Pascal and Montaigne. It differs
from their monumental writings as the nineteenth century
differs from the Roman period, or the middle age. It is
less massive, but it is far more opulent. Emerson is
rarely sublime like Marcus Aurelius, but he disposes of a

wealth of varied illustration of which Marcus Aurelius knew nothing ; and he has turned every page of the book of Nature, which, until these latter ages, it has been the fault of ethical writers to neglect.

Were we to look for the conductor of the Emerson orchestra, we should perhaps find it in the essay entitled " The Over-Soul." It seems to set the music to which the others march. It enforces the ideas which draw all else after them—that the universe is one existence by virtue of its interpenetration by a single divine essence, and that one soul animates all mankind. " We see the world piece by piece, as the sun, the moon, the animal, the tree ; but the whole, of which these are the shining parts, is the soul. . . . From within or from behind, a light shines through us upon things, and makes us aware that we are nothing, but the light is all. What we commonly call man, the eating, drinking, planting, calculating man, does not, as we know him, represent himself, but mis-represents himself. Him we do not respect, but the soul, whose organ he is, would he let it appear through his action, would make our knees bend. When it breathes through his intellect, it is genius ; when it breathes through his will, it is virtue ; when it flows through his affection, it is love. . . . All reform aims, in some one particular, to let the great soul have its way through us." Starting from this postulate, the writer works his way through a number of beautiful illustrations to Carlyle's conclusion, " All history is sacred." The possible exaggeration of this pantheistic optimism into absolute apathy is warded off by a supplementary discourse on Compensation, point-ing out the "inevitable dualism that bisects nature," and

which is reproduced in every separate existence, and every
fact of the spiritual and intellectual life. "If the good
is there, so is the evil ; if the affinity, so the repulsion ; if
the forces, so the limitation." The world is not, therefore, a monotonous effluence of Divinity ; but it is an
effluence nevertheless : and by nothing is the fact proved
more clearly than by the nice adjustment and absolute
balance of compensation throughout the whole of it. It
is an utter fallacy to imagine that the bad are successful,
that justice is not done now.

> " Hast not thy share?　On winged feet,
> Lo ! it rushes thee to meet :
> And all that Nature made thine own,
> Floating in air or pent in stone,
> Will rive the hills and swim the sea,
> And, like thy shadow, follow thee."

The object of the fine essay quaintly entitled " Circles "
is to reconcile this rigidity of unalterable law with the
fact of human progress. Compensation illustrates one
property of a circle, which always returns to the point
where it began. But it is no less true that around every
circle another can be drawn. "The life of man is a
self-evolving circle, which, from a ring imperceptibly
small, rushes on all sides outwards to new and larger
circles, and that without end. Hence all forms of culture,
however relatively perfect, become in time obsolete. For
the genius that created them creates now something
else." Hence there is no security but in infinite progress. " As soon as you once come up with a man's
limitations, it is all over with him. Infinitely alluring and

attractive was he to you yesterday, a great hope, a sea to swim in ; now you have found its shores, found it a pond; and you care not if you never see it again."

Emerson followed his own counsel ; he always keeps a reserve of power. His theory of "Circles" reappears without the least verbal indebtedness to himself, in the splendid essay on Love. Here, having painted as hardly any other has painted, the beauty of personal relations and the "mighty ravishment" of the passion of love, he rebukes his own raptures by treating it as after all something rudimentary, ancillary and preparatory to the liberal use and the perfect knowledge of life, Nature's lure to a higher end, "only one scene in our play." "At last they discover that all which at first drew them together— these once sacred features, that magical play of charms— was deciduous, had a prospective end, like the scaffolding by which the house was built ; and the purification of the intellect and the heart, from year to year, is the real marriage, foreseen and prepared from the first, and wholly above their consciousness." Notwithstanding the assurance that "we need not fear to lose anything by the progress of the soul," this deliverance can hardly act otherwise than as a drench of cold water to the "fine madman" whom the writer, himself performing the part which he attributes to Nature, has allured to this sober conclusion by the bait of gorgeous and impassioned speech. It is, therefore, with all its poetry, rather for the mature than the young.

> " The gay enchantment is undone :
> A gentle wife, but fairy none."

The austere stoicism of the companion essay on Friendship

may affect even the mature reader with something of a
similar jar.   Here, however, it is the general drift that
wounds, and the conclusion that redeems.   "These things
may hardly be said without a sort of treachery to the relation.   The essence of friendship is entireness, a total magna-
nimity and trust.   It must not surmise or provide for
infirmity.   It treats its object as a god, that it may deify
both."   "Self-Reliance" and "Heroism" are another
pair of essays, the former of which must have had especial
influence in shaping the social type then growing up in
New England.   We must pass by these, as well as "Prudence," "Intellect," and "Spiritual Laws," to devote a
word to "History" and "Art."   These illustrate what
an abstract principle, if just in itself, will do for the
elucidation of a given subject, and how far it fails in the
absence of special study. XIn the essay on History we
feel that Emerson's view of human nature as an incarnation of the Divine Spirit binds all the ages together, and
makes them all equally living and real to the man of to-
day, in so far as his knowledge of them supplies colour
for the mental picture.   But we also feel that Emerson
does not personally get much beyond his grand generalization, and that he is indifferent to the archæological
research which is needed for a just realization of the past,
which would have saved him from many fanciful extravagances.   In the essay on Art the fundamental conception of Art as an educational process, elevating the
soul to the perception of beauty, is valuable if not ex-
haustive ; but in concluding that the perception, once
attained, would supersede the educational process and
render art obsolete, Emerson overlooked the fact that

many men are born with physical and mental aptitudes impelling them to artistic employment, and which can find no other exercise. Man must continue to paint and carve, and cultivate music, or the finer endowments of his sense will become as atrophied as the naturalist's relish for Milton and Shakespeare.

Carlyle repaid his obligations to Emerson by a preface to the English edition of the Essays, which secured it immediate recognition in this country. He was evidently not entirely in sympathy with Emerson's literary manner, which he criticizes with justice as abrupt and fitful, nor does he repeat the verdict of his private correspondence on its characteristic merits. These he had already defined with inimitable felicity as "brevity, simplicity, softness, homely grace, with such a penetrating meaning, soft enough, but irresistible, going down to the depths and up to the heights, as silent electricity goes." The public expression of his admiration is mainly reserved for the moralist, the man of sure intuition. "One man more who knows and believes of very certainty that Man's Soul is still alive, that God's universe is still godlike, that of all Ages of Miracles ever seen, or dreamt of, by far the most miraculous is this age in this hour." He had said to like effect in a private letter : " Once more the voice of a man ! Ah me ! I feel as if in the wide world there were still but this one voice that responded intelligently to my own : as if the rest were all hearsays, melodious or unmelodious echoes. My blessing on you, good Ralph Waldo ! " The book's sale in England was at first slow, but its reception in intellectual circles was never doubtful. Milnes, wrote Carlyle, was warm, and

Harriet Martineau enthusiastic. John Sterling, he added, scolded and kissed, as the manner of the man was, and concluded by asking whether it was possible to obtain the author's likeness. By and by lovers began to buy the volume in duplicate, and, having marked their favourite passages in one copy, to lend the other to the beloved one in hopes that she would mark the same; but it was never found to make much difference what she marked. An anonymous critic in *Fraser* classed Emerson among heresiarchs—rightly in the judgment of Carlyle, who described the reviewer as "emphatic, earnest, not without a kind of splay-footed thought and sincerity," and opined that he had enough in him to warrant his holding his peace for the next five years.

Emerson's generosity in the republication of Carlyle's works and the conduct of "The Dial" was the more magnanimous as the situation of his affairs was not brilliant. He had married with a modest competency, but expenses had multiplied, and he could only meet his obligations by lecturing. Lecturing was not then the gainful profession it has since become ; nor had Emerson attained the popularity which attracts lookers as well as hearers, reinforcing those who come to hear by those who come to see. A course of ten lectures which it had taken months to prepare might bring five hundred dollars in Boston ; the county lyceum could only afford ten dollars a lecture with travelling expenses. Even when Emerson got a windfall he was admonished of the truth of Goethe's saying that the trees are not permitted to grow into the sky. "I crowed unto myself on the way home on the strength of my three hundred dollars earned in New York and Providence. But the Atlas Bank declares no dividend ; so I find myself pretty nearly where I was before." Pure literature was not then a pursuit eminently conducive to a livelihood in America ; nor did Emerson understand or care to make the most of it. "The pains," says Mr. Cabot, "he gave himself with bargaining and with book-sellers' accounts for Carlyle, and the common sense he always showed in practical affairs, have sometimes given the impression that he was a shrewd man of business. But in bargaining for himself he was easily led to under-value his own claims and take an exaggerated view of those of the other party, and so usually bought dear and sold cheap." It must be forgiven to a poet that he bought a piece of land to prevent his view being obstructed, and a field in which he had been accustomed to walk lest a new proprietor should turn him out, and a pine-grove lest the old proprietor should cut it down. All this made lecturing doubly necessary that he might continue "to raise his own blackberries." The consideration of some of the most important of his discourses at this period will be best reserved for a review of his relation to national politics. In one of a course on "The Present Age" he put the religious tendencies of the age into a sentence : "Religion does not seem now to tend to a *cultus*, but to a heroic life." In another he dwelt on the narrowness of temperance reformers, and all such as would regenerate society by special nos-trums ; which he exhibited with even more terseness in a passage in his diary written about this time. "You take away, but what do you give? Mr. Jefts has been preached into tipping up his barrel of rum into the

brook; but day after to-morrow, when he wakes up cold
and poor, will he feel that he has somewhat for somewhat?   If I could lift him up by happy violence into a
religious beatitude, or imparadise him in ideas, then I
should have greatly more than indemnified him for what
I have taken."   "The Method of Nature" (1841) was
composed, he says, in the heat and happiness of what
he thought a real inspiration, as it certainly was.   It is
one of the most eloquent and most pregnant of his
productions, a glowing rapture of idealistic Pantheism, a
paraphrase of Goethe's pithy text:

> " Natur hat weder Kern noch Schaale :
>   Alles ist Sie mit einem Male."

"The method of Nature cannot be analysed.   The
new book" (hear this, ye ultra-Darwinians!) "says, ' I
will give you the key to Nature,' and we expect to go
like a thunderbolt to the centre.   But the thunder is
a surface phenomenon, makes a skin-deep cut, and so
does the sage.   The rushing stream will not stop to be
observed : it is the characteristic of insanity to hold
fast to one thought, and not flow with the course of
Nature.   Nature can only be conceived as existing to
a universal and not a particular end, to a universe of
ends, and not to one.   She knows neither palm nor
oak, but only vegetable life.   We can point nowhere
to anything final; but tendency appears on all hands;
planet, system, constellation, total nature is growing
like a field of maize in July."   Possessed for the time by
the divine ecstasy he describes, Emerson recommends
Nature's method as a model for frail man in language
of unsurpassed splendour, and with arguments and

illustrations appropriate to a state of inspiration, but which might well seem extravagant in colder moods. Notwithstanding some golden sayings fit for any time and place, such as " Do what you know, and perception is converted into character," the discourse should as a whole only be read as it was spoken, in the choicest hour. One is not much surprised that the worthy Baptist minister who presided on occasion of its delivery prayed that the audience might be preserved from ever again hearing such transcendental nonsense. Emerson asked his name, and remarked : " He seems a very conscientious, plain-spoken man."

The second series of Emerson's essays appeared in 1844. It may be described as generally dealing with matters of more immediate practical concern than the first had done, as more ethical in spirit, and less rich in imagination. There is, notwithstanding, no lack of poetry in it, any more than of ethic in its forerunner. " Character " is a discourse on the text, " Character is nature in the highest form." It shows that the recluse of Concord had a sound knowledge of life, and of the conditions necessary for enduring success and true greatness. The essay on " Experience " seems at first a singular discourse for a preacher of righteousness. It must be regarded as an endeavour to atone for previous over-statements by a frank recognition of the unmoral aspects of the universe. " Nature, as we know her, is no saint. The lights of the church, the ascetics, Gentoos, and Grahamites, she does not distinguish by any favour. She comes eating and drinking and sinning. Her dar- lings, the great, the strong, the beautiful, are not children of our law, do not come out of the Sunday School, never weigh their food, nor punctually keep the commandments. If we would be strong with her strength, we must not harbour such disconsolate consciences." The essay is full of the apparent contradictions established by experience, but concludes that experience indefinitely protracted will reconcile all. "Manners" insists on self-reliance and self-respect as the first requisites of good manners, and eloquently describes the function of woman in promoting them. "Our American institutions have been friendly to her, and at this moment I esteem it a chief felicity of this country, that she excels in women. Let her be as much better placed in the laws and social forms as the most zealous reformer can ask, but I confide so entirely in her aspiring and musical nature, that I believe only herself can show us how she shall be served. The wonderful generosity of her sentiments raises her at times into heroical and godlike regions, and verifies the pictures of Minerva, Juno, or Polyhymnia; and by the firmness with which she treads her upward path, she convinces the coarsest calculators that another road exists than that which their feet know. But besides those who make good in our imagination the place of muses and of Delphic Sibyls, are there not women who fill our vase with wine and roses to the brim, so that the wine runs over and fills the house with perfume; who inspire us with courtesy; who loose our tongues, and we speak; who anoint our eyes, and we see? We say things we never thought to have said; for once our walls of habitual reserve vanish, and leave us at large; we are children playing with children in a wide field of flowers. 'Keep us,' we cry, 'in these influences, for days, for weeks, and we shall be sunny poets, and will write out in many-coloured words the romance that you are.' "

As might be expected from a poet, the essay on " Poetry " is of special beauty and significance. The conception of the poet and his mission is of the highest. " Poetry was all written before time was, and whenever we are so finely organized that we can penetrate into that region where the air is music, we hear those primal warblings, and attempt to write them down ; but we lose ever and anon a word, or a verse, and substitute something of our own, and thus miswrite the poem." The sign and credentials of the poet are that he announces " that which no man foretold." " He is the Namer, or Language-maker. Each word was at first a stroke of genius. Language is fossil poetry." " He re-attaches things to nature and the whole." " Readers of poetry see the factory-village and the railway, and fancy that the poetry of the landscape is broken up by them—for these works of art are not yet consecrated in their reading ; but the poet sees them fall within the great order not less than the beehive or the spider's geometrical web. Nature adopts them very fast into her vital circles, and the gliding train of cars she loves like her own." [1] Hence the

---

[1] "Just then the train, with shock on shock,
　　Swift rush and birth-scream dire,
　　Grew from the bosom of the rock,
　　And passed in noise and fire.

With brazen throb, with vital stroke,
　　It went, far heard, far seen,
　　Setting a track of shining smoke
　　Against the pastoral green."
　　　　　　　　　COVENTRY PATMORE.

true American poet, when he arrives, will make poetry of the most unpromising subjects :—"our log-rolling, our stumps and their politics, our repudiations, banks, and tariffs, newspaper and caucus, Methodism and Unitarianism;" no less than the northern trade, the southern planting, Oregon and Texas. "Thou true land-lord! sea-lord! air-lord. Wherever sun falls, or water flows, or birds fly, wherever day and night meet in twilight, wherever the blue heaven is hung by clouds or sown with stars, wherever are forms with transparent boundaries, wherever are outlets into celestial space, wherever is danger and awe and love, there is beauty, plenteous as rain, shed for thee, and though thou shouldst walk the world over, thou shalt not be able to find a condition inopportune or ignoble."

Emerson's second series of essays also appeared with a preface from Carlyle, treating this time of the book merely in its aspect of literary property, perhaps because Emerson had apprehended that the former preface might be "too splendid for my occasion. I fancy my readers to be a very quiet, plain, even obscure class—men and women of some religious culture and aspirations—young, or else mystical, and by no means including the great literary and fashionable army who now read your books." Carlyle assured him that his public was truly aristocratic ; being of the bravest inquiring minds that England had. Among these was George Eliot, who wrote of Carlyle's first preface : "This is a world worth abiding in while one man can thus venerate and love another." Emerson's correspondence with Carlyle had been maintained since their first acquaintance, though with occasional fluctuations. Seldom have two men conceived a more genuine and abiding regard for each other on the strength of a single meeting. Emerson betrays that he has been deeply impressed by Mrs. Carlyle also, and is unsuspicious of the negative elements in her character. Carlyle's infirmities of temper come out clearly enough in the correspondence, as also does the deep inward tenderness of his nature. Emerson is always plotting to bring his friend to Concord, and thinks himself so near his object that he inquires whether Carlyle will burn wood or anthracite. But Providence knew better. Carlyle would not have appeared to advantage among transatlantic Transcendentalists; decent civility was all he could achieve towards the individuals of the species occasionally despatched to him by Emerson. It is doubtful whether the precious substance of his lectures would have repaid the American ear for the want of oratorical fluency: and in any event his perversity on the slavery question would have estranged him hopelessly and deservedly from the flower of his audience. Thanks, however, to Emerson in great measure, Carlyle had become an intellectual force in America, and it was natural for New England to pit her seer against her mother's. The contrast between them was exhibited with equal wit and penetration in Mr. Russell Lowell's " Fable for Critics " (1848).

" There are persons, mole-blind to the soul's make and style,
Who insist on a likeness 'twixt him and Carlyle
To compare him with Plato would be vastly fairer,
Carlyle's the more burly, but E. is the rarer;
He sees fewer objects, but clearlier, truelier—
If C's. an original, E's. more peculiar;

That he's more of a man you might say of the one,
Of the other he's more of an Emerson;
C's. the Titan, as shaggy of mind as of limb;
E's. the clear-eyed Olympian, rapid and slim.
The one's two-thirds Norseman, the other's half Greek,
Where one's most abounding, the other's to seek;
C's. generals require to be seen in the mass,—
E's. specialities gain if enlarged by the glass;
C. gives nature and God his own fits of the blues,
And rims common-sense things with mystical hues—
E. sits in a mystery calm and intense,
And looks coolly around him with sharp common-sense;
C. shows you how every-day matters unite
With the dim transdiurnal recesses of night,—
While E. in a plain preternatural way
Makes mysteries matters of mere every day.
E. is rather like Flaxman, lines straight and severe,
And a colourless outline, but full, round, and clear;
To the men he thinks worthy he frankly accords
The design of a white marble statue in words.
C. labours to get at the centre, and then
Take a reckoning from there of his actions and men.
E. calmly assumes the said centre as granted,
And, given himself, has whatever is wanted."

This may be a suitable place to introduce a notice of Emerson's own poetry, as, although "uncertain whether he had one true spark of that fire which burns in verse," he was at this period contributing poems freely to "The Dial," and even entertaining proposals from publishers for a collected edition. The genius of his verse is best characterized by a happy phrase of Dr. Holmes's—it is elemental. It stands in a closer relation to Nature than that of almost any other poet. He has an unique power of making us participate in the life of Nature as it is in Nature herself, not as Wordsworth gives it, blended with

the feelings or at least coloured by the contemplations of
humanity.   Such intimacy with Nature has sometimes all
the effect of magic; there are moments and moods in
which Emerson seems to have as far outflown Wordsworth as he outflew Thomson and Collins.   But the
inspiration is in the highest degree fitful and fragmentary,
and is but seldom found allied with beautiful and dignified
Art. The poems offend continually by lame unscannable
lines, and clumsinesses and obscurities of expression.
Sometimes the poet seems to struggle with more meaning
than he knows how to convey; at other times the meaning
bears no proportion to the laboured intricacy of the diction.   When, however, he is fortunate enough to find the
precise fitting for his idea, the result is a diamond of the
purest water.

> " Not from a vain or shallow thought
> His awful Jove young Phidias wrought ;
> Never from lips of cunning fell
> The thrilling Delphic oracle."

> " The silent organ loudest chants
> The master's requiem."

> " No ray is dimmed, no atom worn,
> My oldest force is good as new ;
> And the fresh rose on yonder thorn
> Gives back the bending heavens in dew."

> " There is no god dare wrong a worm."

> "As the wave breaks to foam on shelves,
> Then runs into a wave again ;
> So lovers melt their sundered selves,
> Yet melted would be twain."

" The musing peasant lowly great
Beside the forest water sate ;
The rope-like pine-roots crosswise grown
Composed the network of his throne ;
The wide lake, edged with sand and grass,
Was burnished to a floor of glass,
Painted with shadows green and proud
Of the tree and of the cloud."

ART.

In the vaunted works of Art
The master-stroke is Nature's part.

GIPSIES.

The wild air bloweth in our lungs,
　　The keen stars twinkle in our eyes,
The birds gave us our wily tongues,
　　The panther in our dances flies.

You doubt we read the stars on high,
　　Nathless we read your fortunes true ;
The stars may hide in the upper sky,
　　But without glass we fathom you.

TO EVA.

O fair and stately maid, whose eyes
Were kindled in the upper skies
　　At the same torch that lighted mine ;
For so I must interpret still
Thy sweet dominion o'er my will,
　　A sympathy divine.

Ah ! let me blameless gaze upon
Features that seem at heart my own ;
　　Nor fear those watchful sentinels,
Who charm the more their glance forbids,
Chaste-glowing, underneath their lids,
　　With fire that draws while it repels.

On the whole, Emerson the poet presents a singular contrast to Emerson the thinker and orator. As the latter he is potent, epoch-making, the morning star of a new era, both literary and intellectual. As a poet he is the lovely, wayward child of the American Parnassùs, more fascinating and captivating than his elders and betters, and nearer by many degrees to the central source of inspiration ; but beautiful rather than strong, and ever in need of allowance and excuse. Could he have always written with the mastery he shows in detached passages, he would have stood in a class by himself. Some few of his poems are actual models of perfection, as, for instance, the lines in the dedication of the Concord monument ; but here, as Dr. Holmes remarks, his originality of style has forsaken him, and he writes in the manner of Campbell. Another noble poem quoted by Dr. Holmes—" Days "— would certainly have been given to Landor if it had not been signed by Emerson. There are, however, pieces of faultless perfection entirely in the Emersonian style. Such a piece is the " Rhodora," worthy of the Greek Anthology :

> " In May, when sea-winds pierced our solitudes,
>   I found the fresh Rhodora in the woods,
>   Spreading its leafless blooms in a damp nook,
>   To please the desert and the sluggish brook.
>   The purple petals, fallen in the pool,
>   Made the black water with their beauty gay ;
>   Here might the red-bird come his plumes to cool,
>   And court the flower that cheapens his array.
>   Rhodora ! if the sages ask thee why
>   This charm is wasted on the earth and sky,
>   Tell them, dear, that if eyes were made for seeing,
>   Then Beauty is its own excuse for being :

> Why thou wert there, O rival of the rose !
> I never thought to ask, I never knew,
> But in my simple ignorance, suppose
> The self-same Power that brought me there brought you."

Almost equally finished, and gushing from a yet deeper well-spring of feeling, is the mystic yet transparent allegory entitled "Two Rivers":

> "Thy summer voice, Musketaquit,
>   Repeats the music of the rain ;
> But sweeter rivers pulsing flit
>   Through thee, as thou through Concord Plain.
>
> Thou in thy narrow banks art pent ;
>   The stream I love unbounded goes :
> Through flood and sea and firmament,
>   Through light, through life, it forward flows.
>
> I see the inundation sweet,
>   I hear the spending of the stream
> Through years, through men, through Nature fleet,
>   Through passing thought, through power and dream.
>
> Musketaquit, a goblin strong,
>   Of shard and flint makes jewels gay ;
> They lose their grief who hear his song,
>   And where he winds is the day of day.
>
> So forth and brighter fares my stream,—
>   Who drinks it shall not thirst again ;
> No darkness stains its equal gleam,
>   And ages drop in it like rain."

Such music and such power of spiritualizing material Nature would have vindicated a high place for a more faulty poet than Emerson : but his claims rest by no means solely even on these high gifts. The Runic, Orphic, mystic, and aphoristic element in his poetry,

though there is too much of it, is still an original and
valuable element. He always means something, and his
meaning is always worth trying to penetrate. Better still,
he always sings something : his verse, good or bad, is
poetry ; he does not, like some greater poets, chequer his
inspired moods with commonplace or mere literary
elegances. But after all it is his greatest glory as a poet
to have been the harbinger of distinctively American
poetry to America :

> " He was the first that ever burst
> Into that silent sea."

Emerson hesitated over the publication of his poems
for four years. He had come, as he said himself, "to a
solstice of the stars of his intellectual firmament," and,
though he retained freshness enough to write " Representative Men " to be noticed subsequently, felt the need
not only for change, but for a more thorough change than
he could find in America. He had pretty well gone
through all the fermentations and combinations of which
American intellectual life was then susceptible, and began
to think that he needed the stimulus of an English
audience. He was dimly conscious of something pro-
vincial in his reputation. The very enthusiasm he had
excited half-frightened him. " In the acceptance that
my papers find among my thoughtful countrymen in these
days, I cannot help seeing how limited is their reading.
If they read only the books that I do, they would not
exaggerate so wildly." With his usual delicacy, he
breathed no hint of his inclination to Carlyle, fearing that
an audience might be artificially collected for him. But

when, in 1846, invitations came from various English Mechanics' Institutes, he accepted them with hope and pleasure. The prime mover was his old friend Mr. Alexander Ireland, "infinitely well affected towards the man Emerson." Feeling himself safe in strong, sure hands, Emerson sailed for Liverpool in the *Washington Irving* (name of fair omen!) October 5, 1847.

CHAPTER VI.

EMERSON, as has been seen, believed in the inward light. He thought a man needed but to keep himself open to the Divine influences to have his life happily moulded for him, and his creed appeared justified by his experience.

> " Early or late, the falling rain
> Arrived in time to swell his grain ;
> Stream could not so perversely wind,
> But corn of Guy's there was to grind."

The Divine blessing, indeed, rarely took in his case the form of money, but intellectual events came as they were wanted, and, unless when in the fulfilment of an obligation of courtesy or conscience he took upon himself some extraneous task like the editorship of "The Dial," everything happened at the right moment for the furtherance of the inner soul and the external end. His well-timed visit to England was a case in point. His celebrity was just in the stage to render him an object of interest, without rendering him an object of adulation. There was enough curiosity respecting him to warrant the best efforts of his devoted friend Mr. Ireland to gain him a hearing, and not enough to tempt a contractor to vulgarize him by "running" him. He came simply and modestly to proffer his thoughts to those who cared for them, and to take in return the impressions derived from the study of a polished society and a social order venerable and stable, yet in process of transformation. England, on her part, was in a more congenial humour towards a man of optimistic faith than she had ever been before, or has ever been since. God forbid that we should be discouraged by anything that has happened since 1847! yet we may admit that the millennium seemed nearer then than it does now. People were not then gravely asking whether life was worth living. The peace of the world, on the brink of such rude disturbance, seemed well-assured. The black cloud depicted with such power in Carlyle's "Chartism" and Disraeli's "Sybil," had lifted off the English working class. By passing the Ten Hours Bill, Parliament had just declared that a man was not a horse. Free Trade had not only been adopted as a political measure, but was thought to have been demonstrated as an economical principle ; and therefore its reception by the whole world seemed but a question of time. It was inconceivable that reasons of State should prevail over reasons of arithmetic—that France and the United States should go on denying two and two to be four, merely because self-interest would have them to be five. Peel was the first man in the country, and Cobden the second. This sanguine faith has since been rudely shaken; the demon has rebuked the exorcist. But were Free Trade to die out of Manchester itself, the fact would remain that its triumph in 1846 was a great

moral victory—the triumph of logic and eloquence. It
had won with everything against it, and its success had
engendered a conviction of the adequacy of moral force
to effect all reforms, and of moral reforms to cure all
physical evils. Peace men, temperance men, ocean
penny postage men, enemies of capital punishment,
friends of Africa and Poland, educationalists, sanitary
reformers, philanthropists, some devoted as Shaftesbury
and practical as Southwood Smith, others in various
stages of lunacy, did incredibly prevail. The very Pope
had set up as a reformer, to the dismay of Prince
Metternich. Lecturing and lecturers were rising nearer
to the American level : the eloquence of W. J. Fox and
George Thompson had won them seats in Parliament,
and George Dawson was beginning to be a power in the
land. Progress was for the time the national watchword,
and it was a real creed and no cánt. Save for the Irish
famine, there seemed scarcely a cloud in the sky when
Emerson made his lecturing arrangements ; he arrived on
the eve of a revolution, and in the middle of a panic.

On landing at Liverpool on October 22nd, Emerson
found an invitation from Carlyle, irresistible as gravita-
tion, he says, in its heartiness and urgency. After
spending some hours with Mr. Ireland in Manchester,
he proceeded to London, and found the Carlyles very
little changed in appearance from their old selves of
fourteen years before. Spiritual progress there had been,
not change, for Carlyle had travelled as steadily on his
own line as Emerson had, and their progress had been in
different directions. They might be compared to two
streams which, rising on the same mountain crest, gush

down opposite steeps, and diverge the more the further
they wend their way. The central idea of each was
alike—the Divine Immanence in all things; but, to
employ Heine's convenient generalization, one presented
it like a Hebrew, the other like a Greek. One note of
Hebraism is intolerance. Carlyle's personal tenderness
to his fellows was profound, but his intellectual anti-
pathies were bitter and fierce, and the serene sage, the
"Gymnosophist sitting on a flowery bank," was among
them. His aversion to Emersonianism equalled his love
of Emerson; it is a proof of the sincerity of his love
that it survived such estrangement. "We had immense
talking with him. here," he writes, "but find that he
did not give us much to chew the cud upon. He is a
pure, high-minded man, but I think his talent is not
quite as high as I had anticipated." At another time he
says, "Good of him I could get none, except from his
friendly looks and elevated, exotic, polite ways." Emerson
could not be expected to shine in conversation with the
first talker of his age; even if, which is improbable, he
was allowed the chance. His was not an exuberant mind.
The habit of nicely fitting his thought with the one right
word in his public utterances made him hesitate in ordinary conversation, and grew upon him until "to hear him
talk," says Dr. Holmes, "was like watching one crossing a
brook on stepping-stones." He the more admired the
affluent discourse of the apostle of Silence, which he classed
as one of the four things that had most impressed him in
Europe. "You will never discover," he told Mrs. Emerson, "his real vigour and range, or how much more he
might do than he has ever done, without seeing him."

This visit to London was short,. but was graced by a social passport in the shape of a breakfast with Rogers, who-received him with the fatigued politeness of one who had provided for all the lions of the last half-century. Returning to Liverpool and Manchester to fulfil his lecturing engagements, he felt oppressed by the gigantic development of industrial life, and shocked by the tragic aspects. of the streets. "My dearest little Edie costs me many a penny. I cannot go up the street but I shall see some woman in rags, with a little creature just of Edie's size and age, but in coarsest ragged clothes, and barefooted, stepping beside her; and I look curiously into *her* Edie's face with some terror, lest it should resemble *mine,* and the far-off Edie wins from me the half-pence for this near one." But he was impressed by the strength, bigness, and solidity of the people, and "a certain fixedness and determination in each person's air that discriminates them from the sauntering gait and roving eyes of Americans. In America you catch the eye of every one you meet, here you catch no eye, almost."

Everything in the provinces went well with Emerson. The Manchester newspapers, distinguished then as now for the excellence of their reports, gave his lectures a wide circulation. Alexander Ireland, though with the care of one of them on his shoulders, "approved himself the king of all friends and helpful agents; the most active, unweariable, imperturbable." Invitations to lecture crowded on Emerson, until he felt ashamed to read yet again "the musty old discourses so often reported." But managers and audiences would have no other. Making Manchester his headquarters, he ranged over all the northern and midland counties, acquainting himself in the most agreeable manner possible with the flower of English middle class culture, and rejoicing in the proof thus afforded that here, as at home, he had beguiled young people into better hopes than he could realize for them. The English railways, he remarked, conveyed him with twice the speed of the American, and half the motion. Perhaps this observation the better prepared him for his meeting with George Stephenson; the more interesting to him in that it brought proof of his doctrine of one soul in many men. No two persons' pursuits could have been more dissimilar than those of the man of speculation and the man of steam. But their minds moved in the same lofty plane of perfect simplicity and sincerity, and in a few moments Stephenson had his hand upon the American's coat-collar, and talked to him of the marvels of electricity and his own engineering experiences, until Emerson declared that it was worth crossing the Atlantic to see him. The great Duke should have been the third man of the party. At Edinburgh, where he went with a lecture composed for the occasion, he met a man as remarkable as Stephenson, but as unlike him as the imagination can conceive. He had formed his conception of De Quincey from the "voluminous music" of his writings, and expected a presence and an elocution "like the organ of York Minster." He saw and heard "a small old man of seventy years (De Quincey was sixty-two), with a very handsome face, expressing the highest refinement; a very gentle old man, speaking with the greatest deliberation and softness, and so refined in speech and manners as to make quite indifferent his extremely plain and poor dress." He afterwards dined at De Quincey's cottage with him and his three admirable daughters, and laments, as we do, that time failed to record the conversation. Jeffrey he found very French and rather affected; and Professor Wilson's lectures to his class seemed to him to call into exercise more strength of body than of mind. Professor Nichol, George Combe, Mrs. Crowe, David Scott, Robert Chambers, and other Scotch notabilities, came within his ken; but his 'chief friend and entertainer was Samuel Brown, then in quest of that Sangreal of science, the demonstration of the unity of substance.

Emerson travelled up to London in the last days of February, with the exciting tidings of the French Revolution ringing all around him. He saw Wordsworth and Harriet Martineau on the road, and on his arrival in town took up his abode with his English publisher, Mr.. (now Dr.) John Chapman, whose house was to harbour George Eliot by and by. Aided by the introductions of the American Minister, he took place at once as one of the conspicuous figures of the London season. His letters home are crowded with the names of the intellectual leaders he had met, the most remarkable exceptions being Browning, then in Italy, and Stuart Mill, who had at this time almost given up society. He seems to have been especially impressed by Leigh Hunt, whom, along with De Quincey, he thought the finest mannered man of letters in England; by Macaulay, in whom he rightly discerned the nearest approximation among them all to the typical Englishman, incarnating the *differentia* of the race; and by Owen, whom he with equal justice pronounced "one of the best heads in England." "Richard Owen," he says in the "Traits," "adds sometimes the divination of the old masters to the unbroken power of labour in the English mind." It is interesting to get a glimpse of him from a Nestor of observation, Crabb Robinson, who writes : "It was with a feeling of predetermined dislike that I had the curiosity to look at Emerson at Lord Northampton's, when, in an instant, all my dislike vanished. He has one of the most interesting countenances I ever beheld—a combination of intelligence and sweetness that quite disarmed me." Miss Martineau had told Robinson that Emerson would not be apprehended till he was seen. "There is a vague nobleness and thorough sweetness about him which moves people to their very depths, without being able to explain why." Robinson agreed that Emerson's first lecture left "a dreamy sense of pleasure, not easy to analyse, or render an account of." Emerson had been lazy about lecturing, and indeed the political circumstances of the times were unfavourable for the promulgation of abstract thinkings. The blaze of Europe threatened to extend to England ; and Chartist and constable were the "representative men" of the hour. At length, however, a course was arranged for the beginning of June, and in the interim Emerson started for a trip to Paris, where he arrived just in time for the abortive revolution of May 15th. The terrible days of June were preparing, but in the meantime Paris showed bravely, crowded with sashes and helmets and men bearded like goats or lions ; full too of living fire, and, as Emerson thought, of genuine passion for justice and humanity. He afterwards said that the French had best discussed what other nations had best done. He had just been inspecting a very different place—Oxford, where seeds of thought were quietly germinating, destined perhaps to produce greater results than the brilliant demonstrativeness of Paris. The new Liberalism was for the moment represented for Emerson by two young men whose fellowships even then hung by a hair—Clough, whom his writings had deeply impressed, and Froude, "a noble youth, to whom my heart warms." Froude was greatly struck by his resemblance to Newman, which is indeed undeniable, and goes deeper than the physical likeness. It is a curious speculation what would have happened if the two could have changed places. Could Newman have found his way to Rome from Massachusetts? What tints would Emerson's spiritualism have imbibed from the painted windows of Oxford? Somewhat later he made a pilgrimage to Stratford-on-Avon with a party from Coventry, among them a very plain young woman who told him that she liked Rousseau's "Confessions" best of all books. He started; then said, "So do I;" and the plain young woman wrote next day that the American stranger was the one real man she had seen. He had had his first and last meeting with George Eliot.

Emerson had all but decided not to lecture in London, but "came to have a feeling that not to do it would be a kind of skulking." He seems to have felt instinctively that, while in the provinces he was heard with serious, almost reverential interest, in London he was only regarded as the last sensation, and the more so the more

aristocratic his audience. He nevertheless paid the
intellectual capital the compliment of preparing three
new discourses on "The Natural History of the Intellect,"
which, with two old ones and that composed for Edinburgh, made up a course under the title of " Mind and
Manners of the Nineteenth Century." He had no
lack of dignified and accomplished auditors, from the
Duchess of Sutherland downwards, but his great pleasure
was in "Jane Carlyle and Mrs. Bancroft, who *honestly*
came." Carlyle also took a lively interest in the course,
and Emerson was pleased to observe how much he was
looked at. The London reporters fell far behind their
Manchester brethren in fulness and accuracy, and though
Emerson writes, "Our little company grows larger each
day," the lectures seem to have produced no great effect
beyond the walls of the Marylebone Institute. Men's
minds, besides, were abundantly occupied with more
exciting themes : and the net pecuniary product was only
£80 instead of the promised £200 : while the high
price of the tickets caused Emerson to be taxed with forsaking the middle class, like the Belgian canons who not
only had to give up their dinners to the bishops, but
were pelted because they had not thrown them out to
the people. He gave three "expiatory lectures—dull
old songs "—in Exeter Hall, and took his leave of the
English platform amid Carlyle's good-humoured laughter
at what he termed the orator's moonshine. But Crabb
Robinson thought it the most liberal discourse that
Exeter Hall had ever heard, and, little suspecting whom
he was hitting, spoke with disdain of those who " shook
their heads at what they could not reduce to propositions

as indisputable as a sum in arithmetic." Mr. Cabot
somewhat doubtfully identifies this lecture with that on
Home, the second of the series on Human Life, delivered
in 1838. The process of thought is not very clear in
the summary, but the conclusion, at which it is hard to
conceive Carlyle smiling, is that of the Essay on Love.
"Man no longer dies daily in the perishing of local and
temporary relations, but finds in the Divine soul the rest
which in so many types he had sought, and learns to
look on them as the movables and furniture of the City
of God." Emerson's last adventure in England was the
expedition to Stonehenge in Carlyle's company, recorded
in "English Traits." On his way from London to
Liverpool he spent a night in Manchester with Mr.
Ireland, and was full of pleasant recollections of his visit
to England. He said he had not been aware "that
there was so much kindness in the world." He sailed
from Liverpool on July 15th, taking a rocking-horse for
his girls and a cross-bow for his son, and was under his
own roof before the end of the month.

Emerson lectured on England in the year of his return,
and again in 1853, but his full impressions were not published until 1856, when they appeared under the title of
"English Traits." In this book he has matched himself
with the English people, and both are upon their trial.
Could an idealist display true insight in dealing with so
practical a nation? Could so material a civilization stand
the criticism of an idealist? England and Emerson both
came well out of the ordeal. He cannot help setting
down the English intelligence as somewhat beefy and
obtuse, for such is the fact. But he does not, like Haw-

thorne, resent the phenomenon as an affront to the foreign
observer: he finds in this stiff soil the substratum of fine
qualities, and boldly declares that the intellect of England owes more to Plato than to Aristotle. The solidity
of the English is no doubt the great primal fact with him.
"I find the Englishman to be him of all men who stands
firmest in his shoes." Practicality, veracity, conservatism, all the traits too plain to be missed, are fully
recognized. But when he comes to literature he pronounces that the two nations in England of whom so
much has been written are not the Norman and the
Saxon, nor the Poor and the Rich, but "the perceptive
class and the practical finality class, ever in counterpoise,
interacting mutually: these two nations, of genius and
of animal force, though the first consist only of a dozen
souls, and the second of twenty millions, for ever by
their discord and their accord yield the power of the
English state." The preponderance of the practical
finality class in his own day is indeed admitted and
deplored. "Even what is called philosophy and letters
is mechanical in its structure, as if inspiration had
ceased, as if no vast hope, no religion, no song of joy,
no wisdom, no analogy, existed any more." "English
science is false by not being poetic. It isolates the
reptile or the mollusc it strives to explain; whilst reptile
or mollusc only exists in system, in relation." This particular reproach has been well-nigh removed from English
science: and in many other departments Emerson would
now find that his hint of "a retrieving power in the
English mind, which makes recoil possible," had been
fully justified. He must also, if Darwin ever engaged his

attention, have had to acknowledge that the recovery of
the lost faculty of generalization came in a great measure
from the very method to which he ascribes its extinction.
"The absence of the faculty in England is shown by the
timidity which accumulates mountains of facts, as a bad
general wants myriads of men and miles of redoubts
to compensate the inspirations of courage and conduct."
The good general often will not move till he has made
his communications safe, and provided for his supplies.

Emerson's book sparkles with epigrams such as these :—
"There should be temperance in making cloth, as well
as in eating. A man should not be a silkworm, nor a
nation a tent of caterpillars." "The lawyer lies *perdu*
under the coronet, and winks to the antiquary to say
nothing." "The upper classes have only birth, say the
people here, and not thoughts. Yes, but they have
manners." "Loyalty is in the English a sub-religion."
"When the Englishman wishes for amusement he goes
to work." "There is in an Englishman's brain a
valve that can be closed at pleasure, as an engineer
shuts off steam. The most sensible and well-informed
men possess the power of thinking just so far as the
bishop in religious matters." Amid all these kindly
sarcasms there is not one sneer : it is plain that our
visitor liked us better than he knew, and did both himself and us injustice when he told Margaret Fuller that
his respect for the Englishman was the more generous
in that he felt no sympathy with him, only admiration.
Carlyle said that "English Traits" was worth all the
books ever written by New England upon the Old ;
and in it England assuredly imported from her descen-

dants much better ware than anything of its class that
she had exported to them, except Sir Charles Lyell's.
Emerson is so little concerned with the fashion of the
day, and so much with the solid foundations of English
life, that his book should endure as long as these do. It
should be a mirror for England to consult from time to
time, and see whether, in gaining the more spiritual look
which Emerson missed, her countenance has lost any of
the frankness and resoluteness which he found. "I see
England," he said in a speech at Manchester, in allusion
to the commercial crisis under which he found the country
labouring — and by republishing his words nine years
afterwards he signified that he had found them true—"I
see her not dispirited, not weak, but well remembering
that she has seen dark days before; indeed with a kind of
instinct that she sees a little better in a cloudy day, and
that in storm of battle and calamity she has a secret vigour
and a pulse like a cannon. I see her in her old age, not
decrepit, but young, and still daring to believe in her
power of endurance and expansion. Seeing this, I say,
All hail, mother of heroes, with strength still equal to the
time; still wise to entertain and swift to execute the
policy which the mind and heart of mankind requires
in the present hour, and thus only hospitable to the
foreigner, and truly a home to the thoughtful and
generous who are born in the soil. So be it! So let
it be! If it be not so, if the courage of England goes
with the chances of a commercial crisis, I will go back
to the capes of Massachusetts, and my own Indian
stream, and say to my countrymen, the old race are all
gone, and the elasticity and hope of mankind must

henceforth remain on the Alleghany ranges, or nowhere."

Accidental as the coincidence may be, his visit to practical England synchronizes with a healthy crisis in Emerson's mind. His discourses on " Representative Men,"
first delivered in 1845, though not published till 1850,
exhibit a greater tendency to the oracular than anything
written before or afterwards. The first lecture, " The
Uses of Great Men," is obscure in the only sense in which
obscurity is justly imputable to Emerson. It is a suc-
cession of sayings, for the most part individually compre-
hensible and sometimes of stimulating freshness, but so
abrupt and discontinuous that we find ourselves landed
at last in Emerson's favourite conclusion with but slight
idea how we have arrived at it. Genius "appears as an
exponent of a vaster mind and will. The opaque self
becomes transparent with the light of a First Cause." It
is the purpose of the remaining lectures to resolve this
pure ray of primal intellect into the sixfold spectrum of
philosopher, mystic, sceptic, poet, man of the world, and
writer; respectively personified by Plato, Swedenborg,
Montaigne, Shakespeare, Napoleon, and Goethe. Here
we find Emerson's success to be proportioned to his hold
on concrete fact. The figure of Plato, of whose per-
sonality so little is known, is, as Carlyle complains, vague
and indefinite. " Can you tell me," asked an auditor of
his neighbour, " what connection all this has with Plato?"
"None, my friend, save in God!" But the other figures
are visible if not palpable. Nothing can be more generous than his trampling down of prejudice in recognizing
the true inspiration of Swedenborg, or more crushing

than his criticism of the merely mechanical element in
that seer. "When he mounts into the heaven I do not
hear its language. A man should not tell me that he has
walked among the angels; his proof is that his eloquence
makes me one." The lecture on Montaigne teaches that
a wise scepticism leads to the same result as a large faith.
" The lesson of life is to believe what the years and the
centuries say against the hours. Things seem to tend
downward, to justify despondency, to promote rogues, to
defeat the just; and by knaves, as by martyrs, the just
cause is carried forward. Let a man learn to look for
the permanent in the mutable and fleeting; let him
learn to bear the disappearance of things he was wont to
reverence without losing his reverence; let him learn
that he is here, not to work, but to be worked upon ; and
that though abyss open under abyss, and opinion displace
opinion, all are at last contained in the Eternal Cause."
The discussion on Napoleon shows Emerson at his best
as a connoisseur of men, and would alone prove that he
did not addict himself to speculation out of incapacity or
contempt for the affairs of the world. The ideologist
judges the man of action more shrewdly and justly than
the man of action would have judged the ideologist; and
after having most brilliantly painted Napoleon's perfect
sufficiency in all things for which virtue is not needful,
puts him on his right footing with, "Bonaparte is the
idol of common men, because he had in transcendent
degree the qualities and the powers of common men."
On Goethe and Shakespeare Emerson says many excellent things, but the former's activity is too multifarious
to be condensed into a lecture, though the man him-

self is got into a sentence: "The old Eternal Genius who built the world has confided himself more to this man than to any other"—and Emerson is incapable of contemplating Shakespeare with the eye of the dramatic artist. His unsatisfied demands ignore the fact that Shakespeare's plays were designed for the stage, and must not be burdened with incongruous wisdom. The marvel is how he has made them carry so much ; and, after all, it may be suspected that in the original representations not a little of what the student most prizes shared the fate of Mr. Puff's description of Queen Elizabeth's side-saddle. Emerson, who afterwards said of Shakespeare, "the greatest mind values him the most," appears in "Representative Men" under concern "that the best poet led an obscure and profane life, using his genius for the public amusement." His criticism thus coincides with the Englishman's observation to Mr. Fields on his visit to Stratford-on-Avon :—"Shakespeare ! who would have cared for Shakespeare if he hadn't written them plays ?"

During Emerson's absence in Europe a literary undertaking had been initiated in which it is to be regretted that he did not see his way to participate. It at that time required the collective exertions of the best minds in America to support a first-class journal which should at the same time be an organ of serious thought. *The North American Review*—since greatly modified—was then cautious, conservative, and quite out of keeping with the aspirations of reformers. To provide them with an organ, *The Massachusetts Quarterly* was established under the direction of Theodore Parker.

Tennyson, in 1830, inscribed a sonnet to a friend who was to be "a later Luther, and a soldier-priest," and was to shoot "arrows of lightning into the dark." Choosing to war with Giant Pagan rather than Giant Pope, the friend became a most eminent archæologist. The poet's prophecy went wandering homeless about the world until it found exact fulfilment in the person of Theodore Parker, who lacked nothing pertaining to the character of Luther, nor superadded anything material. Parker must seem as much less than Luther as the abolition of slavery is less than the Reformation : yet it can scarcely be doubted that in Luther's age he might have played Luther's part. In an age like ours, however, he must inevitably be judged in a great degree by his standing as author and orator, and this is but in the second rank. This incontestable fact is also an incontestable proof of the fallacy of Sir Joshua Reynolds's definition of genius as an infinite faculty for taking pains. This may be an indispensable accompaniment to the thing : it is not the thing itself. Parker's great natural powers were cultivated to the uttermost ; and, in truth, it is hardly possible to name a bookish or oratorical accomplishment that was wanting to him. Vehement, sonorous, copious, terrible in his wrath and moving in his tenderness ; exuberantly imaginative yet severely logical ; erudite yet perspicuous ; ornate yet compact ; he possessed every merit of the orator, while his earnestness delivered him from every defect of the rhetorician. Fine as his parts were, his character was finer : no man so loved God, no man so hated wrong. Yet it is plain that, though his name is indelibly inscribed in the civil and religious history of

New England, it will not endure as that of a theologian or man of letters ; and no reason can be given except a certain second-rateness in the stuff of the mind, the lack of that inscrutable something which stamps Emerson, so greatly Parker's inferior in whatever can be taught, as a man superior in natural endowment. If Emerson was ever tempted to identify genius with character, he might have found the correction of his error in his friend. He seems to have even underrated Parker's gifts, so different to his own. "A little more feeling of the poetic significance of his facts," he said, "would have disqualified him for some of his severer offices to his generation." The main function of the great radical preacher is thus defined with no less truth than eloquence : "His commanding merit as a reformer is this, that he insisted beyond all men in pulpits that the essence of Christianity is its practical morals : it is there for use, or it is nothing ; and if you combine it with sharp trading, or with ordinary city ambitions to gloss over municipal corruptions, or private intemperance, or successful fraud, or immoral politics, or unjust wars, or the cheating of Indians, or the robbery of frontier nations, or leaving your principles at home to show on the high seas or in Europe a supple complaisance to tyrants, it is an hypocrisy, and the truth is not in you ; and no love of religious music, or of dreams of Swedenborg, or praise of John Wesley or of Jeremy Taylor, can save you from the Satan which you are." With this high and just view of Parker's mission, more active co-operation from Emerson in *The Massachusetts Quarterly* might have been expected. He seems to have been annoyed at having been announced as a joint editor without his consent, and perhaps winced under the "one fault" which he finds in Parker. "He over-estimated his friends, and sometimes vexed them with the importunity of his good opinion, whilst they knew better the ebb which follows exaggerated praise." His only contribution was the admirable introductory address (December, 1847), pregnant with ideas then deemed unpractical, but which the recent history of America has made common property. The United States of that day wore in his eyes the aspect of "a certain maniacal activity, an immense apparatus of cunning machinery which turns out, at last, some Nuremberg toys." More pungent criticism of the same kind follows, but Emerson, unlike Carlyle in similar cases, refuses to despair, will not believe that so stupendous a phenomenon as the American Republic can have been called into being for nothing. "Moral and material values are always commensurate. Every material organization exists to a moral end, which makes the reason of its existence. Here are no books, but who can see the continent with its inland and surrounding waters, its temperate climates, its west wind breathing vigour through all the year, its confluence of races so favourable to the highest energy, and the infinite glut of their production, without putting new questions to Destiny as to the purpose for which this muster of nations and this sudden creation of enormous values is made?" The questions with which a journal aspiring to leadership must deal are indicated with admirable exactness, among them slavery, "in some sort the special enigma of the time, as it has provoked against it a sort of inspiration and enthusiasm singular in modern history;" and the adjustment of the balance between "the exact French school of Cuvier and the genial catholic theorists, Geoffroy St. Hilaire, Goethe, Davy, and Agassiz." (Here the wish seems to have begotten the thought, for Agassiz did not belong to Geoffroy St. Hilaire's party.) The life of *The Massachusetts Quarterly* was brief but honourable; it died of superiority to its public within three years. Among its many memorable contributions the only one which concerns us here is Parker's general review of Emerson, a creditable piece of work, bringing out most of Emerson's strong points and by no means sparing his weak ones, his want of logical connection, his occasional inconsistencies and extravagances, his deference to Oriental writers whom in fact he misapprehends. The preponderance of the ethical sentiment in Parker's mind makes him cold to Emerson's mystic absorption in Nature, and the essay is disfigured by a gratuitous comparison of Emerson with a light of the Old World, Milton. But, on the whole, it was a worthy sentence, the first authoritative announcement by an American that his country, at last, possessed a classic.

Another ally of those days, much nearer than Parker, was Henry Thoreau, in whom Emerson took half-paternal, half-fraternal interest, as he had every right to do. Without him Thoreau might never have existed as the hermit-poet of Walden. He had had him in his house two years (1841–1843), and so moulded the young man, not previously deemed over-susceptible to intellectual influences, that Mr. Haskins started with amazement when he found his former classmate "in the tones and inflections of his voice, in his modes of expression, even in the hesitations and pauses of his speech, the counterpart of Mr. Emerson." He adds indeed : " After conversing with Mr. Emerson for even a brief time, I always found myself able and inclined to adopt his voice and manner of speaking." Hawthorne probably had this metamorphosis in mind when he drew Thoreau on one side of his nature as Donatello in his " Marble Faun." Thoreau adopted more than Emerson's manner and tones : he worked out his creed of the sufficiency of the individual, and demonstrated that it is easy to live according to nature in the neighbourhood of a civilized and corrupt society : but, so far at least as his experiments went to show, in such neighbourhood only. " Thoreau's experiment," says Mr. Lowell, " actually presupposed all that complicated civilization which it theoretically abjured. He squatted on another man's land ; he borrows an axe ; his boards, his nails, his bricks, his mortar, his books, his lamp, his fish-hooks, his plough, his hoe, all turn state's evidence against him as an accomplice in the sin of that artificial civilization which rendered it possible that such a person as Henry D. Thoreau should exist at all." But whatever affectation may have infected his method of life, the testimony of his friends, and, better still, of his own writings, forbids the belief that it went further. " To hold intercourse with him," wrote Hawthorne, " is like hearing the wind among the boughs of a forest tree ; and with all this wild freedom, there is high and classic cultivation in him too." There is even higher testimony to the charm of his character in the elevating effect which the remem-

brance of it wrought upon Emerson when he penned
Thoreau's funeral tribute. Hardly any of his writings
have so much natural magic, or such captivating simplicity, down to the noble peroration, itself simple: "It
seems a kind of indignity to so noble a soul that it should
depart out of Nature before yet he has been really shown
to his peers for what he is. But he, at least, is content.
His soul was made for the noblest society; he had
in a short life exhausted the capabilities of this world;
wherever there is knowledge, wherever there is virtue,
wherever there is beauty, he will find a home."

On July 16, 1850, Margaret Fuller Ossoli was drowned,
with her husband and child, on her return from Italy,
after sitting for twelve hours on the stranded wreck
amid driving rain, in sight of the coast and of sundry
persons too diligently picking up whatever came ashore
to busy themselves in procuring a lifeboat. To find such
another contrast of dying or dead genius in presence of
dull, soulless inhumanity, we must go to memoirs of the
"realistic" school of biography. Emerson exclaimed,
" I have lost my audience ! " He could not honestly say
more, for his nature and Margaret's, though by no means
antipathetic, were hardly congenial. Her part had been
that of the ardent mistress, and his the cold beauty's. Failing in her attempts to gain his confidence by storm, she
cried, " Why do I write thus to one who must ever regard
the deepest tones of my nature as those of childish fancy
or worldly discontent ? " Emerson could never feel at
home outside his own sphere, whether of thought or
affection : it was impossible, therefore, that there should
not be something of constraint in his portion of the

biography which, two years after Margaret's death, appeared as the joint production of her most intimate friends. Yet, having helped himself, by reminiscences of conversation and quotations from correspondence, over the intellectual region of Margaret's nature, into which he entered but imperfectly, he kindles up when at last he comes to the generous helpful woman, who went straight from a wedding to attend a relative undergoing a surgical operation, and who, when in after years she found scope for the exercise of all her love and devotion in Italy, "came to it as if it had been her habit and her natural sphere."

Two visitors from Europe about this time have given us glimpses of Emerson. Arthur Hugh Clough, his host at Oxford, his companion at Paris, and in whom he had found (but he cannot have sought very diligently) the only Englishman who put Wordsworth at the top of the modern English Parnassus, having gone through a spiritual revolution in England and looked political revolution in the face abroad, came by his invitation to Massachusetts in search of a quiet haven in which to anchor, and temporal provision upon which to wed. Better provision was shortly found at home, and the translation of Plutarch's "Morals," on which the exiled scholar had been working at Harvard, was finished on this side of the Atlantic. The iconoclast who profanely called Walden "a wood with a prettyish pool," "more and more recognized Emerson's superiority to everybody he had seen. Energy is a very common thing; reasonableness is much less common, and does ten times the good." Another European guest, less to Emerson's taste, was Frederika Bremer, who, carrying the war into Africa, avenged the indiscretions of American tourists by repaying them in kind. There is little harm but exaggeration, however, in her magniloquent account of Emerson, who is alternately a lion and an eagle. The picture of him at Alcott's conversation parties, to which "ladies were invited without distinction of sex," tolerant of rude interruption and quietly embanking the flood of talk, is decidedly interesting. Emerson's manner on such occasions was admirable. To a child of nature who resisted every hint to take his hat off in the drawing-room, he remarked, "We will continue our conversation in the garden." Miss Bremer carried off his "strong, beautiful head" in her album, where Crabb Robinson afterwards saw it. It should be sought for in Sweden.

Emerson's correspondence with Carlyle went on meanwhile with no diminution of cordiality, rather increase, for Carlyle's heart smote him when he thought upon his brusqueness. "Of one impression," he wrote, "we fail not here : admiration of your pacific virtues, of gentle and noble tolerance, often surely tried in this place "— Chelsea, not London. "Representative Men" he pronounces "a most finished, clear, and perfect set of engravings in the line manner "—a neat example of a compliment sheathing a criticism.

CHAPTER VII

THE vein of originality which the man of genius brings into the world must in process of time be exhausted. Well for him if external circumstances or inward resources help him to a new lease of inspiration. In trying to evolve new ideas from his mere brain, Carlyle but exaggerated the old ; historical themes restored to him the freshness of his youth. Emerson confesses the infrequency of original thoughts after his return from Europe ; but as invention waned, his intellectual activity found a new stimulus in a quickened interest in public affairs. Banks and tariffs had given place to questions involving the most momentous problems of law and morality. Emerson was cradled into politics by wrong, as other men into poetry. The Fugitive Slave Law was to him for a decade what for one brief fiery moment the oppression of the Indians had been in 1838. His general attitude towards politics, ere political issues had become absolutely vital and all-absorbing, is thus defined by himself in the address prefixed to *The Massachusetts Quarterly—*

" Lovers of our country, but not always approving of the public counsels, we should certainly be glad to give good advice in politics. We have not been able to escape our national and endemic habit, and to be liberated from interest in the elections and public affairs. Nor have we cared to disfranchise ourselves. We are more solicitous than others to make our politics clear and healthful, as we believe politics to be nowise accidental or exceptional, but subject to the same laws with trees, earths, and acids."

This characteristic aphorism is at the root of all Emerson's thinking in political and social questions. The creed of the Conservative of his dialogue is his own also. " The system of property and law is the fruit of the same mysterious cause as the mineral or animal world." But so is the tendency which is always undermining this system. "The party of Conservatism and the party of Innovation have disputed this world ever since it was made." Their respective claims are set forth in his discourse, " The Conservative " (1841), with such fairness that while the author's personal leanings are evidently to the Liberal side, the Conservative case seems advocated with the more energy and point. Each case, nevertheless, is unanswerable from its own point. of view; but the disputants are admonished that "each is a good half, but an impossible whole." The combination of these irreconcilable moieties is attempted in " Man the Reformer" (1841). The answer is that of the poetic enthusiast. All things are possible to Love. " Let our affection flow out to our fellows ; it would operate in a day the greatest of all revolutions. Let us begin by habitual imparting. Let us understand that the equitable rule is that no one should take more than his share, let him be ever so rich. Let me feel that I am to be a lover. I am to see to it that the world is the better for me, and to find my reward in the act. Love would put a new face on this weary old world in which we dwell as pagans and as enemies too long, and it would warm the heart to see how fast the vain diplomacy of statesmen, the impotence of armies and navies, and lines of defence, shall be superseded by this unarmed child." These generous views had their dangers; combined with Emerson's faith in the individual, they at one period went near to make him an Anarchist. In his oration on "The Young American" (1844) he observed that "Government in our times is beginning to wear a clumsy and cumbrous appearance." In the essay on Politics, published in the same year, he expressed surprise that no one had steadily denied the authority of the laws on the ground of his own moral nature—a hint taken by Thoreau. It was but consistent that he should ridicule "the terror of old and vicious people, lest the union of these States be destroyed. The wise and just man will always feel that he stands on his own feet; that he imparts strength to the State, not receives security from it ; and that if all went down, he, and such as he, would quite easily combine into a new and better constitution." This excessive individualism, partly founded on a hasty assumption of the decay of the State from the extent to which its work was getting to be done by private associations, was sharply checked by the emergence of the slavery question. Emerson could not help discovering that the wise and just were impotent in this matter as individuals ; and that the solution which he rightly deemed most fit could only be obtained by the action of the State. He wished America to follow the example of England by combining compensation with emancipation. " Here," he said, " is a right social or public function which one man cannot do, which all men must do. We will have a chimney-tax. We will give up our coaches and wine and watches. The churches will melt their plate. The father of his country shall wait, well pleased, a little longer for his monument; Franklin for his; the Pilgrim Fathers for theirs, and the patient Columbus for his. The merchants will give; the needle-women will give; the children will have cent societies. Every man in the land will give a week's work to dig away this accursed mountain of sorrow once and for ever out of the world." This was justice and therefore statesmanship. Unfortunately, not only was there little disposition on the part of the North to give, but there was none on the part of the South to receive. It is a shrewd remark of Arbuthnot's, that all political parties die at last of swallowing their own lies. The slaveholders had gone on asserting the divinity of slavery until they believed it. Their growing insolence and brutality, culminating in the attempt to strangle free suffrage in Kansas, and the ruffianly assault on Charles Sumner in the Senate House as he sat writing at his desk, made Emerson an Abolitionist. He had clung to conservatism as long as possible. The annexation of Texas (1845) had not perturbed him; he saw it to be inevitable, and was content if his own State held fast her integrity. Even in resisting the Fugitive Slave Law (1850) he had said, " We will never intermeddle with your slavery, but you can in no wise be suffered to bring it to Cape Cod or Berkshire." The South had now made this attitude impossible, but her truculence seemed to Emerson pardonable in comparison with the moral torpor of his own beloved Massachusetts. He was himself twice hissed at public meetings by descendants of the Pilgrim Fathers. Smarting with grief and shame, he, for a time, forgot his accustomed moderation, lauded John Brown's incendiarism, and appeared to blame the judges for not assuming the functions of legislators. At last, however, the attack on Fort Sumter made everything right. Upholders and antagonists of slavery shook hands over the Union ; the logic of events converted every loyal citizen to emancipation as at least a sound military measure ; and, as Emerson said, "The wish that never had legs long enough to cross the Potomac can do so now." He himself, now as good a civic patriot as anybody, was ever ready with speech and song. "Voluntaries," pieces written to encourage the young to enlist for the war, contain this noble stanza—

> " So nigh is grandeur to our dust,
> So near is God to man,
> When Duty whispers low, *Thou must*,
> The youth replies, *I can*."

Emerson's earnest feeling on the civil war comes out in his letters to Carlyle. Writing in December, 1862, in the midst of deepest discouragement all around, he stoically says : " We must get ourselves morally right. Nobody can help us. 'Tis of no account what England and France may do." But sympathy was ever precious to him ; and even when the fortune of war had so greatly changed as had come to pass by September, 1864, he implores it as fervently as ever: "How gladly I would enlist you with your thunderbolt on our part! How gladly enlist the wise, thoughtful, efficient pens and voices of England ! We want England and Europe to hold our people staunch to their best tendency. Are English of this day incapable of a great sentiment ? Can they not leave cavilling at petty failures, and bad manners, and the dunce part (always the largest part in human affairs), and leap to the suggestions and finger-pointings of the gods, which, above the understanding, feed the hopes and guide the wills of men ?" Alas ! to form a correct opinion on any subject, a nation must know something about it : and the English people, mean-ing well as they always do, were disgracefully ignorant of foreign politics, as they always are. Emerson himself had learned much, and found himself more in sympathy than he had ever expected to be with the stern philosophy of Carlyle. "I shall always respect war hereafter. The waste of life, the dreary havoc of comfort and time, are overpaid by the vistas it opens of Eternal Life, Eternal Law, reconstructing and upholding Society." On Carlyle's wild sally against the American cause, Emerson observes the silence of disdain or compassion. He may have been more lenient from a confession he himself had been con-strained to make. "Everybody has been wrong in his guess, except good women, who never despair of an ideal Right." If, however, the women had this faith, they had partly caught it from Emerson. Making a poet's use of the laying of the submarine cable, he had grandly written in 1857 :

" Be just at home ; then write your scroll
    Of honour o'er the sea
And bid the broad Atlantic roll
    A ferry of the free.

And henceforth there shall be no chain,
    Save underneath the sea,
The wires shall murmur through the main
    Sweet songs of Liberty.

The conscious stars accord above,
    The waters wild below,
And under, through the cable wove,
    Her fiery errands go.

For He that worketh high and wise,
    Nor pauseth in His plan,
Will take the sun out of the skies
    Ere freedom out of man."

Was he conscious of the echo of Campbell in the last stanza ?

The just, necessary, and glorious war for the Union, had, nevertheless, like cathartics in general, many obnoxious accompaniments—among them the temporary impoverishment of Emerson. There was no demand for literature, none for lectures, no dividend on his investments, no return from his wife's property, no purchaser for the wood-lot which, though he declared that his spirits rose whenever he entered it, he would now have sacrificed if he could. In time things righted themselves; and in justice to his son, who was intended for the medical profession, he allowed his old friend Mr. Abel Adams to defray the cost of Edward's college course. For many winters lecturing had been a main dependence, and he had gone further afield in quest of audiences, extending his tours as far as St. Louis. Most of the lectures de-livered on these expeditions appear with alterations in "The Conduct of Life," and others of his later collec-tions of addresses. The Western people took kindly to him : and the fee was sometimes in proportion to the hardship and discomfort involved. Emerson humorously represents the public as betting him fifty dollars a day for three weeks that he will not go through all manner of indignities every day, and stand up reading in a hall every night; " and I answer, ' I'll bet I will.' I do it and win the nine hundred dollars." It was a happy peculiarity of his physical constitution that he could dispense with food "from morn till dewy eve." His letters are full of reports, too good-humoured to be called complaints, of long journeys and short commons, nights passed on the floor of canal boats, bottomless mud and navigation over fixed ice. "In journeyings often, in watchings often." As he grew older his daughter Ellen came to accompany him, a Mignon of hotel and car, gently interposing between him and the more trying incidents of travel.

Emerson's elocution has been frequently described, and most hearers attest its magical effect. It was, or seemed, the purest natural endowment; if it owed anything to art, it was the *ars celare.* It gave the impression of utter absorption in the theme, and indifference to all rhetoric and all oratorical strategem. Composed and undemon-strative as any listener, almost motionless, except for a slight vibration of the body, seldom even adapting his voice to his matter, he seemed to confide entirely in the

justness of his thought, the felicity of his language, and
the singular music of his voice. " He somehow," Mr.
Lowell says, " managed to combine the charm of unpre-
meditated discourse with the visible existence of carefully
written manuscript lying before him on the desk; and
while reciting an oration strictly committed to memory,
he had the air of fetching inspiration from the clouds."
If these were artifices, they did not seem so. We
have already heard Mr. Haskins's testimony that he
could not be even a short time in Emerson's company
without unconsciously copying his manner. This be-
speaks the strong personal magnetism needed to hold
large audiences by ideas so unfamiliar, stated with such
deficient continuity, and set off by so few artificial graces.
A shrewd judge, Anthony Trollope, was particularly
struck with the note of sincerity in Emerson when he
heard him address a large meeting during the Civil
War. Not only was the speaker terse, perspicuous,
and practical to a degree amazing to Mr. Trollope's
preconceived notions, but he commanded his hearers'
respect by the frankness of his dealing with them. " You
make much of the American eagle," he said, " you do
well. But beware of the American peacock." When
shortly afterwards Mr. Trollope heard the consummate
rhetorician, Edward Everett, he discerned at once that
oratory was an end with him, instead of, as with Emerson,
a means. " He was neither bold nor honest, as Emerson
had been," and the people knew that while pretending to
lead them he was led by them.

Emerson was a connoisseur in style, and said there
never had been a time when he would have refused the

offer of a professorship of rhetoric at his Alma Mater. The secret of his own method is incommunicable ; for it is even truer in his case than in Carlyle's that the style is the man. To write as Emerson, one must be an Emerson. His precepts, nevertheless, may be studied by artists in all literary manners. They seem especially aimed at the crying sin of nineteenth-century authorship, its diffuseness. He insisted on the importance of "the science of omitting, which exalts every syllable." A good writer must convey the feeling of "chemic selection" as well as of "flamboyant richness." One practical counsel is to read aloud what you have written to discover what sentences drag. " Blot them out and read again, and you will find what words drag. If you use a word for a fraction of its meaning, it must drag. It is like a pebble inserted in a mosaic. Blot out the superlatives, the negatives, the dismals, the adjectives, and *very*. And, finally, see that you have not omitted the word which the piece was written to state." In the controversy between classic and romantic art, he took the side of the former, which seemed to him organic, while romanticism appeared capricious. But he did not regard this as a question between ancients and moderns ; the antique was always with us.

The discourses of these later years form three volumes, " Conduct of Life " (1860); "Society and Solitude " (1870) ; "Letters and Social Aims " (1875); the latter collection pieced together in Emerson's old age with Mr. Cabot's aid, by combining passages selected from different lectures, so slight was the logical connection of Emerson's thought. These writings indicate a period of diminished mental activity, but not of decay. They may be compared in this respect to the later works of Wordsworth. The author is not mechanically repeating the inspirations of happier hours, still less endeavouring to simulate originality by extravagance; he has simply, finding his voice less dominant from the summit than of old, compensated for its diminished resonance by a closer approach to his audience. He has not, as he says Shakespeare or Franklin would have done (and Lincoln did), given his wisdom a comic form to attract his Western audiences, but he has descended from the shining heights, and discourses from an ordinary platform with even more calmness and self-possession, if with less of mystic rapture and oracular depth. The burden of his message is ever the same, the all-pervading Deity, the one human soul in every breast, the universality of spiritual laws, the exact correspondence of the moral and material worlds, the inexorable impartiality of Nature, the impossibility of stealing a march on eternal justice, the duty of man to yield up his egotism to the universal Soul, and walk by the inward light. But the joy of discovery is over; instead of the seer, we have the man of practical experience vouching for him. Emerson the old beholds the work of Emerson the young, and finds it very good. Not a precept of the latter but has stood the test. If Emerson had written nothing else than these discourses, his reputation would never have existed; if he had not written them, it would have lacked one pledge of stability.

The father of the Samnite general who had taken the Roman legions in a trap, advised him either to kill them

all or to dismiss them without conditions. This seems
the world's alternative, the former method for choice.
But if the genius will not be killed he suddenly finds
himself adored for work often far inferior to that of
his neglected prime. As it befell Carlyle, Browning,
Mill, so it befell Emerson. It had taken years to
exhaust a small edition of "Nature"; "The Dial" had
been given away or destroyed; he had written in 1859,
"I have not now one disciple"; but in 1860 not a
copy of the "Conduct of Life" could be had within two
days after the publication of the book. So rapid a sale
precluded any deliberate verdict on its merits, and was
in fact not a tribute to the book, but to the author, who
might in a sense be said to have lived and written only
for these forty-eight hours. Fame had at last overtaken
desert, and even outrun her; for, excellent as Emerson's
later works still are, they want inspiration. The tersest
of writers shows some symptoms of garrulity, and
unconsciously evades the trouble of original composition
by a free recourse to anecdote. It is also significant
that, with great occasional exceptions, like "The Sovereignty of Ethics," and "The Preacher," he has least
to say upon the loftiest themes. He writes better on
wealth, culture, eloquence; than on poetry, imagination,
immortality. When, as is sometimes the case, grandeur
is attained in these later writings, it is not the sublime
of poetry, but of ethic. "Every man takes care that
his neighbour shall not cheat him. But a day comes
when he begins to care that he do not cheat his
neighbour. Then all goes well. He has changed his
market-cart into a chariot of the sun." A thought still

more pithily embodied in the precept: "Hitch your waggon to a star."

In 1867 Emerson published "May Day," the most elaborate of his longer poems. In essentials it resembles "Wood Notes," "Monadnoc," and the other earlier pieces in which he had striven to merge his own individuality in Nature's, and to identify himself with the life that "sleeps in the stone, dreams in the plant, wakes in the animal." It exhibits a decided advance on these effusions, being nearly free from harshnesses and obscurities, while the poet's absorption into the general life of Nature is even more complete. Nothing can more perfectly express the intoxication of fine spring weather hurrying the minstrel, sometimes dropping a rhyme in his speed, along in the general frolic of dithyrambic joy:

> " Where shall we keep the holiday;
> And duly greet the entering May?
> For strait and low our cottage doors,
> And all unmeet our carpet floors;
> Nor spacious court nor monarch's hall
> Suffice to hold the festival.
> Up and away ! where haughty woods
> Front the liberated floods :
> We will climb the broad-backed hills,
> Hear the uproar of their joy;
> We will mark the leaps and gleams
> Of the new-delivered streams,
> And the murmuring rivers of sap
> Mount in the pipes of the treen,
> Giddy with day, to the topmost spire
> Which for a spike of tender green
> Bartered its powdery cap;

And the colours of joy in the bird,
And the love in its carol heard ;
Frog and lizard in holiday coats,
And turtle brave in his golden spots.
We will hear the tiny roar
Of the insects evermore,
While cheerful cries of crag and plain
Reply to the thunder of river and main."

From the sensuous revel of teeming life and reckless energy the poet ascends by many passages of beautiful natural description to the spiritual conception of Spring as the earthly type of the renovation of the soul :

" Under gentle types, my Spring
Masks the might of Nature's King,
An energy that searches thorough,
From Chaos to the dawning morrow,
Into all our human plight,
The soul's pilgrimage and flight ;
In city or in solitude,
Step by step, lifts bad to good ;
Without halting, without rest,
Lifting Better up to Best ;
Planting seeds of knowledge pure,
Through earth to ripen, through heaven endure."

The chief defect of this rapturous and most melodious poem, after its occasional looseness of metrical and grammatical construction, is Emerson's usual fault of want of symmetry and coherence, obscuring the development of the thought, which, without this abruptness, would appear apt and natural.

We must travel far back to record the decease of Emerson's venerable mother, who, beautiful in her death as in her life, softly faded out of the world in November, 1853. We have ourselves spoken with those who lovingly remember her gentleness and gentlewomanliness, her sweetness of manner and of voice. No other domestic event is recorded until the marriage of Emerson's youngest daughter, Edith, in 1865, to Colonel William N. Forbes—an auspicious union, which in time placed Emerson above pecuniary anxiety, through the prudent management of his son-in-law. Public honours, meanwhile, were falling fast upon him. In 1863 he was appointed one of the visitors to the Military Academy at West Point, where he attracted attention by his eager curiosity. In 1866 he received the degree of LL.D. from his university, and in 1867 he was chosen orator on Phi Beta Kappa day, "as he had been thirty years before," Mr. Cabot reminds us, "but not now as a promising young beginner, from whom a fair poetical speech might be expected, but as the foremost man of letters of New England." He served from 1867 to 1879 on the Board of Overseers of the University, basking contentedly in the grateful academical environment, but taking little active part in the administration. Once he is recorded to have interfered decidedly, when his casting vote defeated a proposal for exempting the students from compulsory attendance at morning prayers. He would not, he said, deny the young men the opportunity of assuming once a day the noblest attitude man is capable of, that of prayer. It does not seem to have occurred to him that to favour this attitude was one thing, and to enforce it another. In 1870 he delivered a course of sixteen lectures at the University on "The Natural History of the Intellect," "which I know the experts in philosophy will not praise ; but I have the fancy that a realist is a good corrector of formalism." His mind, it is probable, had always been too unsystematic for such a task, and he was by this time incapable of any sustained intellectual effort. He fell back on old material, the most recent being the lectures on " Philosophy for the People," delivered in 1866, and summarized in Mr. Cabot's biography. These seem to have teemed with acute and penetrating remarks, but to have been at most a very modest contribution to so great a theme as the natural history of the intellect. Young in heart as ever, Emerson perceived that he had grown old in faculty, and yielded a cheerful submission to the inevitable dispensation in his swan-song, " Terminus " :

" It is time to be old,
   To take in sail :—
   The god of bounds
   Who sets to sea a shore,
   Came to me in his fatal rounds,
   And said : ' No more !
   No farther spread
   Thy broad ambitious branches, and thy root.
   Fancy departs : no more invent,
   Contract thy firmament
   To compass of a tent.
   There's not enough for this and that,
   Make thy option which of two ;
   Economise the failing river,
   Not the less revere the Giver,
   Leave the many and hold the few.
   Timely wise accept the terms,
   Soften the fall with wary foot ;

12

A little while
Still plan and smile,
And, fault of novel germs,
Mature the unfallen fruit.'

As a bird trims her to the gale,
I trim myself to the storm of time,
I man the rudder, reef the sail,
Obey the voice at eve obeyed at prime:
" Lowly, faithful, banish fear,
Right onward drive unharmed ;
The port, well worth the cruise, is near,
And every wave is charmed."

Emerson might now say, " Good-bye, proud world, I'm
going home," in another sense than when in his youth he
played hide-and-seek with the world in the whortleberry bushes.   A repetition of the 1870 course of lectures
in 1871 had greatly tried him.   Sixty-four miles travel
weekly, with intellectual mischief, as he nervously fancied,
at the end of it.   "I have," he tells Carlyle, " abundance
of good reading, and some honest writing on the leading
topics, but in haste and confusion they are misplaced
and spoiled.   I hope the ruin of no young man's soul
will here or hereafter be charged to me as having
wasted his time or confounded his reason."   A kind
friend, John M. Forbes, the father of his son-in-law,
came to the rescue by carrying him off, April, 1871, as
one of a party of twelve bound on a trip to California.
Mr. Thayer, one of the travellers, has recorded the
incidents of the excursion, and preserved morsels of
Emerson's conversation.   Emerson had brought with
him the manuscript of " Parnassus," a selection, of
poetry he was then preparing for the press; and the cir-

cumstance made his talk run much upon the poets.
" 'Faust' was a destructive poem, it lacked affirmation, he
did not like it." The second part he knew but imperfectly. He had observed the peculiarity of the versifica-
tion of Shakespeare's " Henry the Eighth," and wished
for more light on the problem of its authorship. The
coarseness, as he severely called it, of the Decameron
was made tolerable, not only by the grace and purity
of the language, but by its being steeped in Italian
nature, physical and moral. Machiavelli, he said, wrote
like the Devil, uttering his infernal sentiments with as
much sweetness and coolness as if they were summer
air. Wordsworth and Tennyson were quoted with high
praise : he admired the quality of William Morris's verse,
but deplored its quantity. He spoke highly of Byron as
an efficient poet, observing "there is a sort of scenic
and general luck about him." Imagination was the
solemn act of the soul in believing that things have a
spiritual significance. People had been to him with
scruples about the name of Christian, which he did not
share. He was as willing to be called Christian as
Platonist or Republican. " It did not bind him to what
he did not like. What was the use of going about
and setting up a flag of negation ? " There was never,
deposes Mr. Thayer, a more agreeable travelling companion ; he was always accessible, cheerful, sympathetic,
considerate, tolerant ; and there was always that same
respectful interest in those with whom he talked, even
the humblest, which raised them in their own estimation. The incidents of the trip, indeed, were nowise
trying to the temper. The almanac, Emerson told

Carlyle, said April, but the day said June; the country was covered with greenhouse flowers, and every New England bird had a gayer counterpart.   All California's lions roared for Emerson—the Yosemite cataract, the Sequoia grove, the sea-lions of San Francisco, and Brigham Young, now not again to roar for any one.   But the crown of the journey was perhaps the "Alta California's" character of Emerson's discourse on immortality, repeated in San Francisco :—"All left the church feeling that an elegant tribute had been paid to the creative genius of the Great First Cause, and that a masterly use of the English language had contributed to that end."

On the morning of July 24, 1872, Emerson was waked by the crackling of fire, and saw a light in the closet, which was next the chimney.   Unable to reach the fire, he ran down partly dressed to the front gate, and called for help.   His cries were heard, the neighbours came running from all sides, but the wooden tenement could not be saved.   Books, manuscripts, and furniture were almost entirely rescued by the clever promptitude of the townsmen.   They were removed to the Court House, where a study was fitted up for Emerson; the houseless family found a refuge at the Manse, where he had lived before his marriage.   He had taken cold, suffered for some days from an attack of low fever, and, attention being naturally drawn to the failure of memory from which he had already begun to suffer, this was commonly attributed to the shock, incorrectly in Mr. Cabot's opinion.

Excudent alii spirantia mollius aera.   The glory of the United States is public spirit : a feeling as finely displayed towards men of whom the country is proud as in the case of municipal improvements or charitable foundations. Americans set to work to repair Emerson's misfortune as they would have addressed themselves to restore the Capitol. Mr. Francis Cabot Lowell called, chatted, and went away, leaving behind him a letter which was found to enclose a cheque for five thousand dollars, the gift of himself and a few others. Between eleven and twelve thousand dollars more were subscribed, conveyed to Emerson with perfect delicacy, and acknowledged by him with perfect grace. "The list of my benefactors," he said, "cannot be read with dry eyes or pronounced with articulate voice. I ought to be in high health to meet such a call on heart and mind, and not the thoughtless invalid I happen to be at present." He was indeed terribly shaken: his friends deemed a thorough change to the Old World desirable, and in October a thousand and twenty dollars more were presented to him for that purpose. "I am a lover of men," said Emerson, "but this recent wonderful experience of their tenderness surprises." Accompanied by his daughter Ellen, he sailed on October 28th—

> " To see, before he died
> The palms and temples of the South."

Egypt was his goal, but he passed through England, France, and Italy. In London he saw Carlyle, "who opened his arms and embraced me. We had a steady outpouring for two hours and more on persons, events, and opinions." "It's a happiness to see Emerson once more," said Carlyle. "But there's a great contrast between him and me.   He seems very content with life, and takes much satisfaction in the world.   It's a very striking and curious spectacle to behold a man in these days so confidently cheerful as Emerson."   Though Emerson came from the land of Rip Van Winkle, he eulogized the good, strong sleep he got in England, and in general took things most easily throughout his tour, enjoying all the fine scenery that came in his way, and not going a step out of his way for anything. Egypt he found "good and gentle, if a little soporific. These colossal temples, scattered over hundreds of miles, say, like the Greek and like the Gothic piles, 'O ye men of the nineteenth century, here is something you cannot do, and must respect.'"   On his return he spent a pleasant fortnight with Mr. Russell Lowell in Paris ; and the list of new acquaintances he made in England includes Mr. Gladstone, Mr. Browning, and Mr. Ruskin.   He thought Mr. Ruskin the model lecturer, but his pessimism worse than Carlyle's, for there was no laugh to clear the air.   He went to Milton's grave, and inquired, "Do many come here ?"   "Yes, sir, Americans !"   After visiting friends at Oxford, Stratford-on-Avon, and Durham, he fitly concluded his travel by two days spent under the roof of the oldest and staunchest of his English intimates, Mr. Alexander Ireland.   Returning to Concord, a surprise awaited him.   As the engine approached the station it sent forth a note of triumph, peals of bells responded from the town, and Emerson, escorted with music between files of smiling schoolchildren, found his house rebuilt, and every book and every picture in its wonted place.

Emerson had long been a queened pawn; he had
advanced from a humble pulpit to a rostrum whence he
could speak *urbi et orbi.* He was now something more,
a public institution. All took a pride in him ; and wherever he went in his own part of the country he was tended
by an invisible body-guard, vigilant lest the forgetful old
man should take hurt in boat or car. He was deeply
touched by the kindness of apparent strangers. " Perhaps
there should not be the word stranger in any language,"
he said. Englishmen had wished to assist in rebuilding
his house, but he declined, feeling that his own countrymen had done enough. Scotch admirers nominated him
for the Lord Rectorate of the University of Glasgow, where
he was opposed by no less a competitor than Disraeli,
and succumbed to the purer Caucasian. Carlyle had
beaten Disraeli on a like occasion, but Carlyle was at
hand to deliver a speech. He still occasionally wrote, or
gave a public reading : in 1876 he went as far as Rich-
mond to speak before the University of Virginia, unwilling
to refuse an invitation which seemed like an overture of
reconciliation to the North. His last books were " Parnassus," an extensive selection of poems, published in
1874, including, it was thought, many pieces better
adapted for recitation than for perusal ; and the compila-
tion from his later writings entitled " Letters and Social
Aims." It had been promised to a London publisher
when his powers were more equal to the tasks of selection, excision, and combination ; for hardly any lecture
appeared as originally delivered. His inability to fulfil
his engagement was for long a sore trouble, of which he
was relieved by the assistance of his future biographer,

Mr. J. Elliot Cabot, whose self-denying spirit he had celebrated in the lines entitled " Forbearance ":

> " Hast thou named all the birds without a gun ?
> Loved the wood-rose, and left it on its stalk ?
> At rich men's tables eaten bread and pulse ?
> Unarmed, faced danger with a heart of trust ?
> And loved so well a high behaviour
> In man or maid, that thou from speech refrained,
> Nobility more nobly to repay ?
> O be my friend, and teach me to be thine ! "

After the completion of his task, Mr. Cabot would go up at intervals, so long as Emerson continued to read lectures, " for the purpose of getting ready new selections from his manuscripts, excerpting and compounding them as he had been in the habit of doing himself. There was no danger of disturbing the original order, for this was already gone past recovery." On the whole, therefore, Mr. Cabot seems disinclined to print any more lectures, and probably his resolution is wise. When thus engaged, Emerson would take him out for afternoon walks, or bring him into his study for a nocturnal chat—a bright ghost, the shadow of his former self, but sound in body, and retaining perfect clearness of ideas, only afflicted with failure of memory and a frequent inability to fit his speech to his thought. His conversation ran on happy themes, the progress and wonderful discoveries of the age, the admirable persons he had known from Channing downwards, the surprising virtue of the people of Concord, great and small. In one of his latest letters to Carlyle he says : " A number of young men are growing up here of high promise, and I compare gladly the social poverty of my youth with the power on which these draw." As late as 1878 he traversed the western part of the State of New York in a fruitless search for a young mechanic, who had written him a grateful letter, but had questioned his optimism. His last public appearance of importance was at the fiftieth anniversary of the Unitarian Church at Concord, New Hampshire, which was within one day of the same anniversary of his first marriage at that very church. He went to see the house in which his bride had lived, but could not find it. No wonder; it had, American fashion, been moved bodily, but existed still,— emblem of the speaker's faculty. He shared in the commemoration proceedings by reading a hymn, undisturbed by the difficulty he found in following the printed text.

Even in 1881 Emerson spoke on Carlyle's death before the Massachusetts Historical Society, and on "Aristocracy" before the Concord School of Philosophy. In this last year of his life we obtain a glimpse of him from Walt Whitman, who, on a visit to Mr. Sanborn, and afterwards at Emerson's own house, noted him as a silent but apparently attentive listener to conversation, "a good colour in his face, eyes clear, with the well-known expression of sweetness, and the old, clear-peering aspect quite the same. A word or short phrase only when needed, and then almost always with a smile."

In February, 1882, Longfellow died, and Emerson, a friend of fifty years' standing, went to the funeral. "The gentleman who lies here was a beautiful soul," he said, "but I have forgotten his name." A few months before he had said to a visitor : "When one's wits begin to fail, it is time for the heavens to open and take him away."

This aspiration was fulfilled on April 27, 1882, after a few days' illness from pneumonia. " In these last days in his study his thoughts often lost their connection, and he puzzled over familiar objects. But when his eyes fell on a portrait of Carlyle that was hanging on the wall, he said, with a smile of affection, " *That* is the man, my man." When confined to his bed, "he desired to see all who came. To his wife he spoke tenderly of their life together and her loving care of him ; they must now part, to meet again and part no more. Then he smiled and said, "Oh, that beautiful boy ! "

Seldom had "the reaper whose name is Death" gathered such illustrious harvest as between December, 1880, and April, 1882. In the first month of this period George Eliot passed away, in the ensuing February Carlyle followed; in April Lord Beaconsfield died, deplored by his party, nor unregretted by his country ; in February of the following year Longfellow was carried to the tomb; in April Rossetti was laid to rest by the sea, and the pavement of Westminster Abbey was disturbed to receive the dust of Darwin. And now Emerson lay down in death beside the painter of man and the searcher of Nature, the English-Oriental statesman, the poet of the plain man and the poet of the artist, and the prophet whose name is indissolubly linked with his own. All these men passed into Eternity laden with the spoils of Time, but of none of them could it be said, as of Emerson, that the most shining intellectual glory and the most potent intellectual force of a continent had departed along with him.

CHAPTER VIII.

THE man in Emerson is easily pourtrayed, not so the author. Other thinkers on his level have usually been more or less systematic. They have, in Emersonian phrase, " hitched their waggons," not to a star, but to a formula, to which their thoughts converge, and around which these may be grouped. But Emerson's want of system is the despair of the natural historian of philosophy, and if we place him rather upon the roll of poets, we are still unable to remove him from the roll of anomalies. Nor can the chronological method be applied to him. A literary activity. extending over the third of a century usually implies development, modification, restatement and recantation, an earlier and a later manner. Emerson never sang a palinode, never made a new departure, took no old ideas back, and put no new ideas forward. He did indeed apply his principles more freely to politics and ordinary affairs ; " chemic selection," moreover, gains more and more the upper hand of "flamboyant richness " in his later style. But with these abatements, and apart from the evidence of date occasionally afforded by historical allusions, he has left little that he might not have written at any time of his life.

Renouncing, therefore, the endeavour to give a connected view of Emerson's writings, we will briefly enumerate some of the respects in which he is most original and remarkable.

More than any of the other great writers of the age, he is a Voice. He is almost impersonal. He is pure from the taint of sect, clique, or party. He does not argue, but announces; he speaks when the Spirit moves him, and not longer. Better than any contemporary, he exhibits the might of the spoken word. He helps us to understand the enigma how Confucius and Buddha and Socrates and greater teachers still should have produced such marvellous effects by mere oral utterance. Our modern instructors, for the most part, seem happily born in an age of print, and labour under singular obligations to Dr. Faustus. With Emerson the printing press seems an accident : he uses it because he finds it in his way, but he does not need it. He would have been a light of the age of Buddha or of Solon, as well as of ours.

He is a characteristically American voice. He precisely realizes the idea which the American scholar ought to set before him. American literature must not be feeble and imitative. It is vain to transplant a million cultivated Englishmen across the Atlantic, if they think and speak exactly like those who stay at home. But neither must American literature be conceited and defiant, a rebel against rules founded in the eternal fitness of things. Two and two make four on both sides of the Atlantic. "A Kosmos," if you will, but not "one of the roughs." Emerson's attitude is perfect, manly and independent,

slightly assertive, as becomes the spokesman of a literature on its trial. "Meek young men grow up in libraries,
believing it their duty to accept the views which Cicero,
which Locke, which Bacon, have given; forgetful that
Cicero, Locke, and Bacon, were only young men in
libraries when they wrote those books." He puts the Old
World under contribution; he is full of verbal indebtedness to its philosophers and poets; but what he borrows,
that he can repay. His thoughts continually repeat Plato
and Goethe; but every competent reader perceives that
it is a case of affinity, not of appropriation. Poetical and
religious minds will think alike: it would nevertheless
have made little real difference to Emerson if Plato and
Goethe had never lived. But it would have made a
great difference to this American if Washington had never
lived. He was thoroughly possessed with the ideas of
the Declaration of Independence, and when some one
sneered at them as "glittering generalities"—"Glittering
generalities!" cried Emerson indignantly, "they are
blazing ubiquities!"

Further, Emerson is an important figure in American
literature, as continuing, supplementing, and combining
two of the principal among American thinkers, parted but
for him by an immeasurable abyss. It will have sufficiently appeared from the citations already made that
Emerson's thought rests upon two sure pillars—God and
man—God, "re-appearing with all his parts in every moss
and cobweb;" Man's soul "calling the light its own,
and feeling that the grass grows and the stone falls by
a law inferior to and dependent on its nature." The
first is the idea of the greatest of New England reasoners,

Jonathan Edwards, the Spinoza of Calvinism. "God and real existence," said Edwards, "are the same." "God is, and there is none else." As, however, he retained all the tenets of Calvinism, " he is," says Mr. Leslie Stephen, "in the singular position of a Pantheist who yet regards all nature as alienated from God. Clearing away the crust of ancient superstition, we may still find in Edwards writings a system of morality as ennobling, and a theory of the universe as elevating, as can be discovered in any theology." This "clearing away" was the very operation which Emerson, whose study may have been but little in Jonathan Edwards, did nevertheless virtually perform on his system :

> " He threw away the worser part of it,
>   And lived the purer with the other half."

His connection with Channing on the side of humanity is as intimate as his connection with Edwards on the side of Divinity, and his obligation is far more direct and personal. The special distinction of Channing is his enthusiastic assertion of the dignity of man, a mean animal in the estimation of most theologians. Emerson, as we have seen, thought that he owed little to Channing's conversation, but he imbibed the speaker's spirit at every pore. His magnificent claims for man as the organ of the Universal Soul are but Channing's humanitarianism quickened and sublimed by alliance with Edwards's Pantheism. When Channing told George Combe that "he did not think much intellect was necessary to discover truth ; all that was wanted was an earnest love of it ; seek for it, and it comes of itself somehow," he gave

Emerson a text to "write large." "The soul is in her native realm, and it is wider than space, older than time, wider than hope, rich as love. Pusillanimity and fear she refuses with a beautiful scorn ; they are not for her who putteth on her coronation robes, and goes out through universal love to universal power."

Next to religion, morals. Here Emerson's special characteristics are manifold. The most important are summed up in Matthew Arnold's brief and exquisite character of him as "The friend and aider of those who would live in the spirit." Arnold compares him to Marcus Aurelius, to whom the same character is equally applicable. Mr. Thayer, nevertheless, is right in observing that Emerson is Aurelius and something more. "Marcus Aurelius was not a man possessed. Emerson was. His morals are not merely morals, they are morals on fire." Add to this that Aurelius is not an optimist : or at most his optimism is that of acquiescence and resignation ; while Emerson's is that of the morning stars singing together, and the sons of God shouting for joy. His faith (for, after all, optimism is a plain inference from the existence of God) has brought upon him more objurgation than all his heresies. Theologians are distressed at his imperfect realization of evil and sin : that uncomfortable personage, Henry James, senior, doubts if he can have had so much as a conscience, seeing that, unlike James himself, he attained the age of fourteen without the slightest temptation to commit a murder : Carlyle saw in him "a gymnosophist sitting on a flowery bank." Mr. Morley, to whom death is "a terrifying phantom" and life "a piteous part in a vast drama," naturally finds "his eyes sealed to at least one half of the actualities of nature and the gruesome possibilities of things." As regards the "possibilities," Emerson would perhaps have replied by his own stanza :

> " Some of your ills you have cured,
>   And the sharpest you still have survived ;
> But what torments of pain you endured
>   Erom the evils that never arrived ! "

As respects the "actualities," the case is stronger, but Emerson never said that all existing things were the best, but that they were for the best. He insists that all things gravitate towards the good, and that this progression is infinite ; which, if we look back only as far as the time when the worm first essayed "to mount the spires of form," seems an irrefragable conclusion. From the moral indifference often justly chargeable upon optimists of Oriental type, Emerson is protected by the Marcus Aurelius element in his constitution. He cannot be accused of making the ways of virtue too easy. His writings are full of the loftiest lessons of renunciation. He it was who wrote :

> " Though love repine and reason chafe;
>   There came a voice without reply :—
> 'Tis man's perdition to be safe,
>   When for the truth he ought to die."

"It is in vain," he says, "to make a paradise, but for good men. The resources of America and its future will be immense only to wise and virtuous men." "When you shall say," he warns the scholar, "as others do, so will I ; I renounce, I am sorry for it, my early visions ; I must eat the good of the land, and let learning and romantic expectations go until a more convenient season : then dies the man in you; then once more perish the buds of art, .and poetry, and science, as they have done already in a thousand thousand men." The man," he says elsewhere, "who renounces himself, comes to himself." [1]

Politics, being -but applied morals, come next under review : and here too Emerson was original and significant. Like Carlyle, he was in this department very weak as well as very strong : and even his strength was chiefly as a protest against certain evil tendencies of his day. Carlyle's paradoxical glorification of despotism had the merit of forcing into strong relief the most pernicious features of the time, the cowardice of rulers, the weakness of authority, the general disposition to make words do duty for deeds. Emerson's extreme assertion of individual right, which would have logically resulted in the dissolution of the State, was still valuable as a counteractive of one of the most mischievous features of American politics, the tendency to swamp all individuality in party organization, controlled in the last resort by the cunning and the base. Those Republicans who on occasion of the late Presidential election broke the "Machine" by preferring their country to their party, were probably not unacquainted with Emerson's writings, and were at all events such men as his writings were meant to produce. Like Carlyle's, Emerson's extravagance eventually corrects

---

[1] An excellent analysis of Emerson's ethics, and indeed of all his essential characteristics as a thinker, will be found in "The Religion of the Future," by Mr. J. B. Crozier.

itself : no nation could travel long on the road prescribed
by either of them without a sharp recall.   Emerson himself came to see that "easy good-nature had been the
dangerous foible of the Republic."   This admission is
from his oration on the death of President Lincoln : the
peroration of which is one of the best instances of the
grandeur he attains when, rising above the local and
temporary in politics, he deals with the essential and
eternal :—

"The ancients believed in a serene and beautiful Genius
which ruled in the affairs of nations, which, with a slow
but stern justice, carried forward the fortunes of certain
chosen houses, weeding out sinful offenders or offending
families, and securing at last the firm prosperity of the
favourites of heaven.   It was too narrow a view of the
eternal Nemesis.   There is a serene providence which
rules the fate of nations, which makes little account of
time, little of one generation or race, makes no account
of disasters, conquers alike by what is called defeat or
what is called victory, thrusts aside enemy and obstruction,
crushes everything immoral as inhuman, and obtains the
ultimate triumph of the best race by the sacrifice of everything which resists the moral laws of the world.   It makes
its own instruments, creates the man of the time, trains
him in poverty, inspires his genius, and arms him for his
task.   It has given every race its own talent, and ordains
that only that race which combines perfectly with the
virtues of all shall endure."

This maxim of the one special faculty of each race and

each man was a favourite one with Emerson. "A man," he says, "is like a bit of Labrador spar, which has no lustre as you turn it in your hand until you come to a particular angle, then it shows deep and beautiful colours." The illustration conducts us to the field of science, where Emerson's position is again exceptional, and this time of the very strongest. He fills the place which Goethe's death had left void, of a poet divining the secrets of nature by his instincts of beauty and religion. The gates of the temple of modern science turn upon the two main hinges of his thought—real unity in seeming multiplicity; immanent, not external power. Of unity he says, "Each animal or vegetable form remembers the next inferior and predicts the next higher. There is one animal, one plant, one matter, and one force." Of Divine immanence:—"There is a kind of latent omniscience not only in every man, but in every particle. That convertibility we so admire in plants and animal structures, whereby the repairs and the ulterior uses are subserved, when one part is wounded, or deficient, by another; this self-help and self-creation proceed from the same original power which works remotely in grandest or meanest structures by the same design, works in lobster or mite, even as a wise man would if imprisoned in that poor form. 'Tis the effort of God, of the Supreme Intellect, in the extreme frontier of his universe." This is from one of his latest writings: in the earliest he had said: "The noblest ministry of Nature is to stand as the apparition of God. It is the organ through which the universal Spirit speaks to the individual, and strives to lead back the individual to it." No wonder that a natural philosopher who is also a poet—Professor Tyndall—should have written in his copy of " Nature," " Purchased by inspiration."

Nature glides into art by the pathway of beauty, by which art travels back to her. Emerson, as a writer, stands in this middle ground; he is rather a votary of the beautiful than an artist. From his preference for the classical over the romantic school, one would have expected to have found the sentiment of form strongly developed in him. On the contrary, few have been so incapable of fashioning a symmetrical whole. He does achieve it now and then in a short poem, but only by a sort of casual inspiration or mental miracle. His single thoughts are commonly beautifully moulded and exquisitely polished, but they are miniature wholes, not members of a great whole. He rarely tests his constructive faculty by the delineation of a character or the narrative of a sequence of events. What is peculiar to him, and ample recompense for all his defects, is the atmosphere of diffused beauty in which his works lie bathed. They glimmer with a magical light, like twilight air, or the waters of the Concord river in his own beautiful description : " As the flowing silver reached the clump of trees it darkened, and yet every wave celebrated its passage through the shade by one sparkle." This fluid, living, fluctuating beauty, by enveloping the entire composition, makes amends for the want of linked continuity of thought. An essay of his is like a piece of lustrous silk, it changes as the light falls upon it; now one piece chiefly charming, now another; in a flat mind the whole disappoints ; in a genial mood one would say to Emerson, with Emerson :

> " Thou can'st not wave thy staff in air,
> Or dip thy paddle in the lake ;
> But it carves the bow of beauty there,
> And ripples in rhymes the oar forsake."

This general investiture of loveliness is unfavourable to sustained eloquence. When Emerson essays high-wrought passages they are apt to die away, or rather to melt into a lower strain by such gentle gradations that you must look up to see how far you have come down. His isolated fine sayings may be counted and rated like gems : but the pervading beauty of his work has the character which he too absolutely attributes to all beauty ; it is "like opaline doves'-neck lustres, hovering and evanescent." "There is nothing so wonderful in any particular landscape as the necessity of being beautiful under which every landscape lies." This peculiarity makes it difficult to assay and appraise him by quotation ; the water in the vase never seems quite the same as the water in the spring. So far as the charm of his style is communicable, it seems to reside in his instinct for selecting the words which wear the most witching aspect, call up the fairest associations, and most adorn the matter in hand. There could not be a happier instance of "proper words in proper places," than the first two sentences of the address at the Cambridge Divinity School, delivered, be it observed, in June : "In this refulgent summer it has been a luxury to draw the breath of life. The grass grows, the buds burst, the meadow is spotted with fire and gold in the tint of flowers." Any other epithet than *refulgent* would have been a misfit. What effect, too, is conferred upon a simple catalogue of natural phenomena by perfect propriety of diction, every word beautiful, and every word right!

" It seems as if the day was not wholly profane in which we have given heed to some natural object. The fall of snowflakes in a still air, preserving to each crystal its perfect form ; the blowing of sleet over a wide sheet of water, and over plains ; the waving ryefield ; the mimic waving of acres of houstonia, whose innumerable florets whiten and ripple before the eye ; the reflections of trees and flowers in glassy lakes ; the musical, steaming, odorous south wind, which converts all trees to wind-harps ; the crackling and spurting of hemlock in the flames ; or of pine logs, which yield glory to the walls and faces in the sitting room—these are the music and pictures of the most ancient religion."

The subjective writer who imparts his own being freely to his reader—like Burns, or Shelley, or Carlyle, or Emerson—has this advantage over even greater writers—Homer, Shakespeare, Milton—whose themes lie outside themselves, that he can arouse personal affection, and a fond concern for the perpetuity of his fame. " Love," says Emerson, " prays. It makes covenants with Eternal Power in behalf of this dear mate." Throughout Emerson's writings there is not a hint of his subjection to " the last infirmity of noble minds," but it is an infirmity which his lovers and friends must take upon themselves. One reflection occurs immediately : he can never get beyond the English language. He has been excellently translated into German, and even into Italian :

it is, perhaps, within the resources of French prose to provide a better translation still. But no merely French, or German, or Italian reader will have the least notion of the magic of his diction : hardly even will the foreigner well versed in English enjoy him to the full. As regards the durability of his reputation with the English race, Emerson, like most of the great moderns who have written much and lived long, stands in his own light. No more than Goethe, than Wordsworth, than Hugo, has he given us only of his best. The tribunal of letters looks grave, in the persons of Mr. John Morley and of Matthew Arnold. "There are pages," says the former quite truly, "which remain mere abracadabra, incomprehensible and worthless." And even the good is faulty, observes Arnold, with equal truth. Emerson's diction wants "the requisite wholeness of good tissue." Yet even these accusing angels became compurgators, and dismiss Emerson with a passport to posterity. Another kind of immortality, perhaps the only kind which he greatly valued, is his already. He is incorporated with the moral consciousness of his nation. "His essential teaching," says Professor Norton, in a letter to the writer, "has become part of the unconsciously acquired creed of every young American of good and gracious nature." If more is to be claimed for Emerson, as it well may, we should rest the claim, apart from his literary worth, on his impersonation of one of the main tendencies of his time, and his rebuke of another. This is an age of science, and science has found no such literary inter-preter as Emerson. Not only, says Professor Tyndall, is Emerson's religious sense entirely undaunted by the dis-

coveries of science ; but all such discoveries he com-
prehends and assimilates.   "By Emerson scientific
conceptions are continually transmuted into the finer
forms and warmer hues of an ideal world."   While thus
in sympathy with his age where it is right, he is against
it where it is wrong.   It has, as a whole, made the
capital mistake of putting happiness before righteousness.
Utilitarianism has begotten effeminacy, and effeminacy
discontent, and discontent despair.   Posterity will see
in Emerson one man valiant and manly in a repining
age.   A lesser man might earn greatness thus.   The
story is told of shipwrecked mariners on a rock relieved
from fear when the lightning-flash revealed a humble tuft
of samphire, for the samphire is never covered by sea-
water.   Welcome in such a plight the obscure weed,
much more the brilliant flower.

THE END.

INDEX.

www.ingramcontent.com/pod-product-compliance
Lightning Source LLC
Chambersburg PA
CBHW032007060726
47497CB00017B/2362